A GOOD FIGHT

DAVID GURNEY

A Good Fight

Paul's Journal

...ts his moral right to be identified as the author of

...om The New English Bible, Oxford University
...ge University Press, 1970.

ST PAULS Publishing
187 Battersea Bridge Road,
London SW11 3AS, UK

Copyright © ST PAULS 2000

ISBN 085439 604 7

Set by TuKan DTP, Fareham, UK
Printed by Interprint Ltd, Marsa, Malta

ST PAULS is an activity of the priests and brothers
of the Society of St Paul who proclaim the Gospel
through the media of social communication

CONTENTS

I	SUBJECTION	7
II	LIBERTY	11
III	POWER	28
IV	SUBORDINATION	42
V	DEJECTION	55
VI	CHALLENGE	67
VII	RESPONSE	83
VIII	DISCOURAGEMENT	100
IX	MOTIVATION	114
X	STIMULATION	129
XI	REACTION	143
XII	DANGER	159
XIII	OPPORTUNITY	177

For our sons
Andrew, Richard, Nigel

I
SUBJECTION

IT had been one of those days of rare beauty which become markers in the memory, a day in Springtime, bursting with birth, pregnant with the promise of Summer to come. In all of my sixteen years I had never before been so aware of the potency of nature. I had moved through the whole day in silent wonder at the impact upon me of the physical world. As never before, I had heard the songs of birds, seen the colours of flowers, drunk in their scents, noticed the patterns of shadows thrown by trees and buildings, absorbed the all-embracing gold of sunlight, and yielded to the over-arching marvel of the cloudless blue sky. Overwhelmed by so much new awareness, I had avoided human company as much as possible; and now, after thanking my mother for our evening meal, I asked my father's permission to leave the house. Still lost in uncomprehending wonder, I made my way through the streets, now tranquil in the serene light of evening, to the river bank. All the restless activity of the day had subsided, as if in response to the utter stillness of the air. Little fishing boats rested motionless on the placid water. Larger trading vessels seemed to be contemplating their own reflections in the unruffled river. Not a breeze stirred. Sails were all furled and stowed away for the night; no rigging flapped protestingly against restraining masts. Only the occasional call of a sea-mew broke the deep, deep silence crowning the breath-catching beauty of the end of the day. Long thin bars of brown cloud lay along the western sky, their edges glowing with the glory of the brightness behind them. It was as if all the concentrated brilliance of the sun had been released when it sank below the horizon, to flood half the heavens with molten gold, its intensity only enhanced by the upward thrust of the little black masts of the boats moored against the opposite bank of the river.

There were a few people about; but they were still, quiet, subdued by the all-pervading peace of the dying day. Totally captivated by the new experience of heightened awareness, greedily drinking in every fresh sensation presented to my perceptions, I stood at the water's edge, alone. And then not alone. In the almost utter silence I sensed, rather than heard, the merest sound behind me. I swung round. It proved to be my undoing. In a split second I saw Alexander lunging towards me. Then his clenched fist smashed into my face. Thrown off balance, I lurched sideways. As I went down, he hit me as hard as he could in the pit of my stomach, and then started kicking me viciously with his booted right foot; but by then he had lost the advantage of surprise which he had briefly enjoyed. Driven by a primitive survival instinct, I began to give as good as I was getting. I managed to grab his flying foot when it was barely a hair's-breadth away from my nose, and he crashed ignominiously to the ground. Furious at having been caught so completely by surprise, I vented my rage on him with all the unrestrained violence that can characterise teenagers teetering on the verge of manhood. Although Alexander had the advantage of me in the matter of size, we were more or less evenly matched in strength; and I knew I was the more agile of the two of us. We rolled around on the ground for some minutes, each desperately trying to get the better of the other, grunting, gasping, mouthing the foulest obscenities about each other, until, with one superhuman exertion, I succeeded in pinning him face down on the ground, sitting astride him with both his arms held firmly in my grasp.

Of course, I knew what all this was about. My father had been married and widowed before he met my mother; and Alexander was his son by his first wife. Initially my mother had agreed to care for him as a full member of the family; but the loss of his own mother had obviously scarred him deeply. We had co-existed amicably enough to begin with; but as we developed, we had diverged from each other. Disagreements degenerated into rank irrational hostility – we both asserted our individuality in terms of our differences from each other. Our mutual animosity became so intense as we moved into adolescence that my mother's natural kindheartedness eventually snapped under the strain. After one particularly bad bout of unrestrained malevolence between us, she suddenly burst into floods of tears, turned to my father and, declaring that she could tolerate it no longer, pleaded with him to expel her stepson from the house. To everyone's utter amazement, my father complied; and by nightfall Alexander was out on the street, with literally nothing more than the clothes he stood up in, and his sleeping mat rolled up on his shoulder. As he left, his face white with shocked disbelief, he hissed at me, "You bastard – I'll get even with you for this."

As I struggled to keep my advantage over him, I regained sufficient self-control to reflect that I shouldn't have been too surprised at what was happening; but then my face flushed again with anger at the suddenness and ferocity of his attack on me. Mastered now by cold hatred, I pushed him savagely over, kneed him in the groin with all the force that I could muster, and, taking advantage of his acute agony, I half-lifted, half-kicked, him, down the river-bank into the water. There was a splash; then nothing more. I looked around. No one seemed to have noticed anything, no one appeared to have heard anything. I straightened out my clothing, dusted my hands clean, and walked away.

Years, decades, later, in Rome, I endured bitter and sustained opposition from a coppersmith. His name was Alexander.

II
LIBERTY

TO this day I do not know whether my family were aware of what happened on that landmark evening in Tarsus, on the banks of the river Cydnus. On balance I think they were not; but I remember breaking out in a cold sweat when, very shortly afterwards, my father announced that he was sending me to Jerusalem to further my education. With what I now recognise as an irrational reaction arising from a feeling of guilt, I was seized by the thought that this could be a veiled reference to a course of correction, even a punishment, for a sin so heinous in the eyes of my family that it could only be referred to indirectly, under colour of another development.

For heinous it certainly was – or so it seemed to me. My upbringing had been strict, very strict – and I was proud of the fact. I consider myself to be a Hebrew of the Hebrews; I am a member of the tribe of Benjamin, and my father had taken meticulous care to observe all the requirements of the Law. A Pharisee himself, he had rigorously trained me to keep all the traditions of the Elders; and I drew great inner strength from the conviction he had instilled into me, that I had been chosen to obey the whole of the Law, in every last particular, without diminution or deviation. But now debilitating doubt began to plague me. What had I done? With increasing insistence it bore in upon me that I had flouted the Holy Law of very God himself. I agonised miserably with myself for days, weeks, months. Was it so wrong – was it wrong at all – to do something so natural, so instinctive, as to react against attack? – and that not for the mere gratification of my own lust, but because of the overpowering need to preserve my own life? But these weak waves of petulant protest broke ineffectually against the Law's consistent and uncompromising condemnation of violence. I could not escape the terrifying realisation that at bottom I was guilty of violating the Law itself – that self-same Law which I had been so earnestly taught to revere, honour and obey, as the only way in which I could be accounted acceptable to God.

Then with the brittle arrogance of youth I made a puerile effort to break free of the whole creaking construction of obligation and obedience, of rebellion and retribution. But deep inside me I knew from the outset that the attempt was futile. Young as I was, I realised instinctively that concepts such as righteousness and sin, guilt and justification, were not simply products of my intensely-religious upbringing – they were objective realities, which would not conveniently go away if I merely tried the simple expedient of ignoring them. I could not so easily escape the consequences of exercising my freedom to choose my course of action.

The more I wrestled with these intractable thoughts, the more the word 'escape' insinuated itself into my thinking; and I began to see my father's decision that I should pay an extended visit to Jerusalem as a means of making an escape. Of course, I was in any case at the age when restless youth feels most strongly the desire to be free of the restraints of home. I had outgrown what were initially essential supports, and now saw them only as irksome limitations on my perception of myself as a fully mature independent being. Suddenly I was tired of Tarsus, frustrated by its distance from the sea, irked by the heavy hand of the Roman administration, scornful of the petty rivalries of its provincial society, and now, most of all, alarmed by the influence of its pagan schools and their teachers. But Jerusalem – ah, now, Jerusalem seemed to be in every respect a better proposition: Jerusalem, the stronghold of King David, the Zion beloved of the Psalmist and the Prophets, the guardian of the Temple of Yahweh, the very dwelling place of God himself. It was in Jerusalem alone that the whole array of sacrifice was offered, to propitiate the righteous wrath of God against the wickedness of sin, and to divert his just judgements from the heads of guilty sinners. Surely there, and only there, could my moral turmoil be assuaged, my spiritual torment eased. My father's voice arrested my racing thoughts. "The most precious thing I can give you now, Saul, is this letter." He handed me a sealed bag. "When you reach Jerusalem, make it your first duty to seek out Rabbi Gamaliel, and give this to him. I have asked him if he will accept you as one of his pupils. Our family is not completely unknown to him – I have reminded him that my own father was a student of Hillel, his grandfather."

My prospects seemed to be brightening by the hour. Not only did my father's plans for me chime with my own wishes, but it now seemed as if he was unknowingly easing my search for a solution to my deep dilemma; for if anybody could answer the anguished questioning that racked my every waking moment, surely Gamaliel could. He was one of the most famous teachers of the day. If he could not tell me whether or not I had done wrong, and if so, how I could put it right – or rather, how I could be put right – then no one could. The seething disquiet torturing my thoughts by day and invading my dreams by night, slowly began to subside. I gratefully grasped the rope of hope that had been unwittingly thrown to me, and persuaded myself that I could now begin to discern the possibility of a resolution of my quandary, four hundred miles away, in the city of Jerusalem.

Now my days were filled with purposeful activity. This was to be my first stay away from home. I relished the thought of travel; but now that practical arrangements needed to be made, I experienced an unexpected shift in my perception of things that had only so recently seemed dull and boring. Familiar streets and buildings seemed to exert a pull on me, and I felt a strange, almost emotional, sense of affinity with the distant peaks of the Taurus mountains, far away to the north of Tarsus. They had always been the unnoticed background to the life of every ordinary mundane day; but now that I knew I would be moving far from them, they seemed to exercise an unsettling pull on my feelings. By the time the day for my departure finally arrived, I was distinctly unsure of myself. I did not know whether I would ever return; and I was caught unawares by a lump in my throat and tears in my eyes when I kissed my mother goodbye. I was grateful that she stayed in the house; but I was just as appreciative of the fact that my father accompanied me as far as the town gate before he turned back, and I continued on the road.

I rapidly fell into a routine that made the most of the opportunities and limitations of travel. Though at home I had sometimes been irritated by the restraints of Roman rule, I now appreciated the advantages of their roads. Peasants' lumbering, wooden-wheeled, ox-drawn carts lurched and bumped painfully over the close-laid setts; wealthy merchants' ponderous wagons rumbled along, their drivers shouting and swearing at the slower farm vehicles when they got in their way. Occasionally a light, open two-wheeled gig bowled merrily past, with an officious driver conveying a rich individual, or a covered wagon would pass me, with several fare-paying passengers, and their luggage piled up all around them; and there were always government-licensed self-drive light chariots, available for hire from the posting-houses placed at regular intervals along the roads. The only travellers I could outpace on foot were the government officials and grand ladies being borne along in litters, their bearers sweating profusely in the heat, sometimes preceded and followed by armed guards. In the course of my long journey from Tarsus in the north-east corner of the Great Sea to Jerusalem in the south-east, I experienced most of these forms of transport. I found people were only too willing to talk, to while away the tedium of long hours of travel; but I met no one with whom I felt I could share the heavy perplexity insistently pressing down on me. So I tried to analyse my problem for myself. I deliberately relived, as dispassionately as I could, the events of that unforgettable evening. I attempted a cold dissection of what had happened, and tried to classify the different elements of the whole experience in logically appropriate categories. But it was a futile exercise. I found that I simply could not chop up a seamless whole into disconnected gobbets and look at them in isolation – they persisted in relating to each other, and running back into each other again, hopelessly muddying the clear factual reasoning I was attempting to impose on them. Yet I did not easily give up the struggle. I made a serious and sustained effort to focus my mental powers, not only on recalling what had happened, but also on why I had acted and reacted as I did. What did I actually want to do? Whatever anyone else might think, I knew I genuinely wanted to obey the Law. What had I in fact done? I had shattered it with a high hand and a haughty mien. Why? Why had I done the very last thing I could ever contemplate doing? I could not understand it. What I wanted to do, I did not do; what I hated, I did. Faced with these irreconcilable facts, I was driven to the conclusion that since I had done what I did not want to do, it could not be me who had done it. I had – I still have – the desire to do what is good; but I cannot carry it out. For what I do is not the good I want to do; no, the evil I do not want to do is what I keep on doing. I made one more effort to sustain an intellectual analysis of what I was rapidly coming to realise was a moral issue. I pinned down my conclusions with the thought that there must be an alien law at work within me, decreeing that though I want to do good – though in my inner being I delight in God's law – evil is right there within me as well, waging war against me, making me a prisoner.

It was raining when I finally arrived in Jerusalem. The contrast with my expectations when I first set out could hardly have been greater. I had had no choice but to make the last stage of my journey on foot; and the approach to the city from the north was crowded with gigs and carriages, coaches and wagons, carts, litters, camels, donkeys, mules, soldiers on horseback and countless pedestrians, all loudly demanding priority of passage and the precedence of privilege. The noise all round was intolerable, and the mud and mire and manure underfoot unavoidable. The relentless rain had soaked through my head-dress and cap, and now plastered my hair to my head, my wet clothes clung uncomfortably to my body – and my misery was complete when I felt my right foot coming out of my sandal, which was held immovably in the unspeakable ooze on the ground. The crush of the crowd all around me gave me no chance whatsoever of retrieving it, and I finally made my first entrance into the Holy City filthy, frustrated and fuming at the indignities to which I, a Pharisee, was being so uncaringly subjected. Later that evening, installed in a small but clean and tolerably comfortable guest-room in the city, I reflected ruefully on the unsettling match between my external experience, and my internal condition. Both outwardly and inwardly the blue sky of God was completely obscured by leaden grey cloud bearing down oppressively upon me. Nowhere could I discern a shaft of light to gladden me, a gleam of hope to sustain me; and although a welcome wash and a change of clothes had freed me from physical dirt and discomfort, I found no corresponding release from my moral malaise. Deeply dispirited by the yawning disparity between my expectations of Jerusalem and my experience of it, I cried out to God in spontaneous despair; but the only response was a knock on the door of my room, and an anxious enquiry from my landlady as to whether I was alright.

Next morning I made a determined effort to get a firm grip on myself and my circumstances. A good night's sleep had restored my spirits, and the lowering grey clouds had cleared from the sky. The previous day's rain seemed to have washed the very air clean – it had the sparkle of new wine about it; and every shape and colour in the bustling crowded city impinged on my senses with crystal-sharp clarity. I went to the Temple; and a few discreet enquiries of fellow Pharisees facilitated my introduction to Gamaliel. I made an appropriate greeting, and proffered him the leather pouch my father had given me when I left home. The great man opened it, read the letter inside, and broke into a broad smile. "Young man," he said, "if my grandfather was your father's teacher, I shall be delighted to be yours." That man's perception of God and his ways and his will drew me and held me as a magnet draws and holds iron. My stay in Jerusalem lengthened from weeks into months, and eventually into years. I was able to support myself with the tent-making craft to which my father had apprenticed me in earlier years; but I spent as much time as I could listening to Gamaliel's lectures, discussing what he said with his disciples, and immersing myself in Targum, Teaching and Torah. They were halcyon days. My appetite for knowledge and understanding was only increased by its satisfaction. I exulted in the testing and extending of my intellectual powers; and I wrote proudly to my father when I was elected to membership of the Sanhedrin.

Almost immediately I saw an opportunity to make my mark. A small group of religious eccentrics had recently emerged in Jerusalem. They made a habit of standing in the Temple courts, usually in Solomon's Colonnade, and talking to whoever would listen to them about a man called Jesus. My first information was that he had been executed by the Romans a few years earlier for treason, because he refused to deny the charge that he allowed his followers to call him a king; but when I began to ask questions about his case, an older Pharisee quietly took me to one side and explained that there was considerably more to it than that. Conviction on the political charge of treason had been necessary to secure the occupying power's agreement to the death penalty; but the man's crime had actually been much graver. He had violated the Law by perpetrating blasphemy. Apparently, by means of hints, innuendoes, allusions, he had indirectly but unmistakably implied that he was the long-awaited and imminently-expected Messiah. There was nothing particularly unusual about that, of course; we have had a positive crop of such claimants in recent years, and needless to say, nothing has come of any of them. But my informant went on to say that there had certainly been some out-of-the-ordinary phenomena connected with this Jesus. There had been reports of food and drink being conjured out of thin air, and rumours of storms on Lake Galilee being stilled with a word. There was a steady flow of accounts of people receiving instant and complete cures from a whole range of disabilities – and not just in the north, where the man originated from, and had built up a widespread and excited following. Some alleged healings in Jerusalem itself had been closely investigated by the religious authorities, who had professed themselves unable to account for them in any rational way. Up to that point I had been intrigued, but not overly-concerned, by what I was hearing; but when my colleague started talking about dead people being restored to life, I assumed that this particular manifestation of Messiah mania had taken off on flights of fancy which freed me and every other level-headed person from any need to concern ourselves with it any longer. I said as much to my friend. He fixed me with a grim expression. "If only that were possible," he muttered darkly, going on to explain that Jesus' friends and followers, so far from being cowed by the loss of their leader, were now confidently asserting that he himself had risen from death, and that this was proof of the truth of his claims. Worse than that, they were, with breathtaking impudence, attempting to turn the tables on the Sanhedrin by claiming that we, the very people entrusted with the Law, had irretrievably forfeited our privilege by instigating the rejection of God's Chosen One.

It became apparent to me that this needed to be taken a little more seriously than I had at first thought. I decided I should investigate matters for myself, rather than rely solely on the say-so of another, however much I might respect him. So I tore myself away from the rare pleasure of intellectual pursuits, and headed for the vastly-different stimulation of the streets. It did me a world of good. Life in Tarsus had nothing to compare with the heady excitement of Jerusalem. I plunged headlong into the melée of humanity swarming in the city – and realised with a shock of surprise that it was very far from being just the City of the Fathers, as I had been led to believe. Tall Parthians stood out in the crowd, and Medes and Elamites were distinguishable by their related languages; I recognised Mesopotamian dialects mingling with Jewish accents, and felt a spontaneous lift of the spirit when I heard the speech of people from Cappadocia, Pontus, Asia, Phrygia and Pamphylia – provinces bordering my Cilician homeland. There were stately Egyptians and swarthy Libyans, disdainful Romans, shifty Cretans, intelligent-looking Greeks and aloof Arabs, bearing with them the solitude of the desert. And as my ears became attuned to the voices all around me, I began to hear snatches of conversation, mere handfuls of words wafting away on the wind, which seemed to chime obligingly with what I was wanting to hear. I heard talk of the 'Way', and more mentions of the name Jesus than was inherently likely in normal circumstances. My inquisitive instincts were now thoroughly aroused, and I made for the Temple. There sure enough, in Solomon's Colonnade, was a considerable number of people standing and sitting in a sizeable semi-circle around a group of a dozen-or-so others. I sauntered casually to the edge of the crowd, and began to make mental notes. The people at the front were an enigma; their mode of dress and manner of speaking stamped them incontrovertibly as ordinary working men, but they were talking with a confidence and conviction which would have done credit to trained orators. I listened with growing amazement as they spoke with glowing intensity about Jesus of Nazareth. They seemed to be fired with an enthusiasm I had never met before, and an absolute assurance which gave their words an unmistakable ring of authority. In no way were they putting forward tentative propositions for debate; the very first words I heard when I came within earshot were, "Therefore let all Israel be assured of this: God has made this Jesus, whom you crucified, both Lord and Christ." A frisson of consternation ran through the crowd; and as the speaker paused to give his words maximum effect, someone shouted out, "Brothers, what shall we do?" The first part of the reply was not particularly outrageous – "Repent and be baptised, everyone of you"; I had heard that the prophet John had said just that at the height of his hey-day, a few years previously. But my spine tingled with horror at what I heard next – "in the Name of Jesus Christ, so that your sins may be forgiven; and you will receive the gift of the Holy Spirit. The promise is for you and your children, and for all who are far off – for all whom the Lord our God will call."

The speaker went on, but I had heard enough – more than enough. Reeling with shock and anger at the horrifying blasphemy being openly touted in the very courts of the Temple itself, I staggered away, almost blinded by the furious emotion raging within me. This must be stopped, and stopped immediately, before it infected any more gullible common people. But then I almost stopped in my tracks as I realised that I had noticed quite a surprising number of priests in the crowd. Why were they there? It dawned on me that perhaps my indignation had run away with me. Presumably the leaders of the Sanhedrin had arranged for them to be there, in order to let these rash enthusiasts know that they were not going unnoticed. I made a conscious effort to calm myself – I almost smiled to myself with the thought that the defence of the Faith of the Fathers did not rest wholly and solely on my slim shoulders. But then my deep-seated fervour flared hotly again, and I knew I had to throw myself without reserve into the extirpation of this pernicious heresy, regardless of whether or not anyone else was doing anything about it.

I felt better when I was able to analyse my initial reaction to the morning's experience. I even modestly congratulated myself that I had sensed something of the dangers of irrational extremes, and that I was sufficiently in control of myself to think clearly through to a realistic course of action. I decided that the best first step I could take would be to ask for Gamaliel's views and advice on the whole business. As always, that man was a beacon of sanity to the darkness of my turmoil. He suggested to me that we should stand back from this startling phenomenon, and see how it developed. He reminded me that people like Theudas, and Judas the Galilaean, had confidently proclaimed themselves to be the Messiah, and had for a while succeeded in persuading some people to believe them; but one way or another their movements had faded and failed, because they were not genuine. Gamaliel counselled a wait-and-see policy. If the current movement evaporated in the same way, it would prove itself to be bogus; but if by any chance it should be God's long-awaited promised intervention to save his people – Gamaliel needed to say no more. I shuddered at the appalling thought of being found fighting against God.

And yet, and yet... In the cool shade of Gamaliel's room in the Temple precincts, listening to his cultured voice calmly advocating civilised reason, I saw the wisdom of his argument. But only two days later I found myself overwhelmed by the urge to take forceful action against the followers of this Way. Perhaps impelled by a perverse desire to go in search of provocation, or even to foment it if I could not find it, I went again to Solomon's Colonnade. Sure enough, there they all were – if anything, more of them than I remembered seeing before. I recognised some of the faces in the crowd, but no one took any notice of me; everyone was intent on what was happening at the front – and in no time at all, so was I. Seven men were kneeling before twelve others, who were presumably leaders of the group, and who each in turn laid their hands on the heads of each of the seven, and offered prayer, though I could not hear exactly what was said. Then the seven stood and turned to face the crowd, who broke into spontaneous applause, and were clearly approving them. My attention was immediately caught and held by one of the seven. He was a young man, with the added appeal of striking good looks. He stood straight-backed, square-shouldered, and everything about his posture proclaimed youth, health and strength; but it was his face which captivated me. He turned his gaze slowly round the semi-circle in front of him with a smile which revealed perfect white teeth, classically symmetrical features and an impressively-strong profile. There was a radiance emanating from him, difficult to describe, but impossible to miss. He made a discernible impact on the crowd; there was a noticeable stir as people nudged each other and turned to comment to their neighbours. From whispered exchanges around me I gathered that his name was Stephen; and someone actually confided in me, "He's a good man – full of the Holy Spirit, you know." I almost started to ask, "What do you mean – 'full of the Holy Spirit'?" but I checked myself just in time with the thought that the question might mark me out as a non-member of the group, with possibly unfavourable consequences. But the comment only served to heighten the fascination of the man. I watched him closely, and found myself irresistibly drawn to the group's meeting-place, almost every day, and sometimes more than once a day. Stephen's natural charisma seemed to me to develop steadily, and I realised that I could be in danger of being ensnared by it, so I concentrated on what was being said – though I found to my very considerable surprise that there were also some astonishing things being done. A physically fit and active man in his forties was pointed out to me as being without the slightest possible doubt a cripple who had sat for years at the Beautiful Gate of the Temple, begging for alms from pilgrims and passers-by. People insisted that he had been instantly and completely cured by two prominent followers of the Way, who apparently told him, "In the name of Jesus Christ of Nazareth, walk" – and he was alleged to have done exactly that, there and then. This was obviously unusual, but it was certainly not unique –

some of my fellow Pharisees have the power of driving out the evil spirits which cause disease in people's bodies and disorder in their minds. But it was the use of the Name of Jesus – and moreover, coupling it with the sacred title of Christ, the Messiah, the Chosen One – which so distressed me. However attractive the proponents of this new belief might be, however impressive the signs with which they tried to validate their claims, they were promulgating a hideous and damnable heresy, and I soon discovered that I had no difficulty in jettisoning my kindly old teacher's advice. There was now no question in my mind but that this grotesque distortion of the Faith of the Fathers was an affront to the honour of God, and must be nipped in the bud before it could take root and flourish.

Almost immediately events played into my hands. I was not the only one antagonised by the followers of Jesus of Nazareth, or Nazarenes, as they were now tending to be called. The lead in opposing them was now taken up by members of the so-called Synagogue of the Freedmen. To my chagrin, they were not orthodox Jews of Jerusalem, members, as I would have preferred, of my own Pharisee party, but foreigners, brethren of the Dispersion; however, I derived a small crumb of comfort from the fact that they originated from my own homeland of Asia Minor. Fortunately, they picked up on the two most significant features of the Nazarene heresy – its preaching against the Law, and its contempt for the Temple. They also had the good sense to concentrate their attacks on Stephen, who as good as selected himself as the target for their attention by his charismatic character, and his provocative prominence among the Nazarene speakers. So for a time controversy swirled around this one man; but from what I saw and heard I had reluctantly to admit that it was very far from being an equal contest. Outnumbered he certainly was, but by no means was

Stephen outwitted. He seemed to be able to draw on inner reserves of wisdom and fluency which his opponents could not match. The cogency of his argument, and the clarity with which he presented it, consistently baffled them, until in the end they were forced to fall back on persuading men with no great incommoding moral scruples to swear on oath that they had heard him say that Jesus would destroy the Temple and change the customs handed down to us from Moses himself. The charge was of course sufficient for Stephen to be arrested, and the very next day he was duly arraigned before the Sanhedrin, accused of blasphemy, and asked if he had anything to say in his defence.

Begrudgingly, I concede that Stephen's defence was magnificent. Not a seat in the Council Chamber was empty, and not a single extra person could have been crammed into the standing room for the general public; but when the accused began to speak, a silence descended on the whole assembly which was almost tangible in its intensity. Stephen began by taking the traditional line of reviewing the whole history of our people, from as far back as the time of the patriarch Abraham. This augured well for him – as I write these very words, I am surprised by the strength of the persisting memory I have of the sense of sympathy I felt for him at first; and I instinctively knew I was not alone in that. But it all dramatically changed when Stephen's survey reached the reign of King Solomon. Without warning, he suddenly abandoned the safe path he had so wisely trodden up to that point, and launched into stinging criticism – of the whole Jewish people, the Sanhedrin in general, and with what I thought was a defiant toss of his handsome head in my direction, "you who have received the Law but have not obeyed it."

Of course, his doom was sealed from that moment. All hell seemed to break out in the Council Chamber, but the High Priest strove strenuously to maintain some semblance of order in the proceedings; and he was momentarily successful. He secured a brief lull in the storm of shouting and abuse; but with an almost perverse sort of death-wish, Stephen plunged headlong to his own condemnation. Gazing intently upwards, he simply said, with quiet intensity, "Look, I see heaven open, and the Son of Man standing at the right hand of God." There was no restraining the Council now. The High Priest shouted in vain for the proper pronouncement of verdict and sentence – he could hardly be heard above the roar of rage from rulers and rabbis. There was a concerted rush at the prisoner as the whole Sanhedrin seemed to fall prey to a collective abandonment of dignity and decency. Learned teachers of the Law fought fiercely with each other to get close enough to Stephen to slap and punch and kick him; and hands which so reverently handled the sacred scrolls of the Scriptures, roughly ripped his light clothing from him – he was stripped stark naked before he was out of the Chamber, and was savagely lynched as he was pushed and pulled along the street to the nearest gate. There he was lifted bodily high into the air, and to a derisory cheer from the crowd which had inevitably materialised from nowhere, was brutally flung against the city wall. For a moment of eerie uncertainty, nothing happened. With startling incongruity, a flight of white doves swooped overhead. Then Stephen managed to stagger to his feet. Legs apart, facing his tormentors, he slowly lifted his arms above his head and, with his face to the sky, cried out, "Lord Jesus, receive my spirit." Once again, his uncrushed courage triggered his own fate. A strapping hulk of a man standing right next to me stripped to the waist and, bending down, picked up a huge stone. With a roar of rage which seemed to give him super-human strength, he hurled it at the blood-streaked youth, naked and defenceless in the morning sun against the implacable wall. The stone found its mark with a sickening thud. Stephen let out an involuntary cry, and the momentary paralysis of the crowd all around him was released. A storm of flying stones homed in upon him, and he quickly fell to his knees. From my position at the front of the imprisoning crowd I heard him gasp, "Lord, do not hold this sin against them." Then yet another grisly missile split his head open, and he slumped to the ground. There was no sound from him now, no more movement. A few more stones were thrown, but now they could make no difference. The mood of the crowd suddenly changed. The furious hatred which had energised it all through the drama was completely dissipated. People began to turn their backs on the ugly sight, and with curious self-conscious embarrassment, moved away from the scene, as if wishing to give the impression that they had not actually been there. I stooped to pick up the clothes of the men whose testimony had led to Stephen being arraigned in the first place. As I did so, I realised with a pang of horror that I was repeating a movement I had already made that morning; for I too had bent down and picked up a jagged-edged stone and hurled it with venomous hatred at the brave young follower of Jesus.

III
POWER

THERE was thunder in the hills around Jerusalem that night. Summer lightning flickered fitfully under lowering storm clouds; but no rain gratified parched fields, or sweetened dusty streets. I drifted restlessly between uneasy sleep and confused wakefulness, unable next morning to distinguish between the two. By then the weather had cleared, and the day dawned as bright and warm as usual; but my spirits failed dismally to rise with it. I felt weighed down by an oppression which was almost physical, but was also more than physical. Moody and irritable, I spurned the usual bread and honey, cheese, dates and olives prepared each day by my landlady, and wandered disconsolately through the unfeeling city. I neither knew nor cared where I went. When the strident strife of the streets stressed me beyond bearing, I sought sanctuary in secretive side-alleys and peaceful-seeming passageways; but these always seemed only to open out again into busy bazaars or crowded market-squares. I was conscious of an impulse to search, though I knew not for what; I was aware of a need to find, but I was unable to satisfy it. As the day wore on I trudged ever more wearily in the enervating heat, until it slowly dawned on me in the late afternoon that I had unwittingly worked my way round to the Temple on the east side of the city. My mood perceptibly lifted, and I wondered why I had not gone there in the first place; here at least I would be able to find tranquillity, and perhaps also the opportunity to bring some sort of order to my disorganised thoughts and feelings. Hope fed on encouragement, and I began to sense the possibility of bringing my mind and emotions under disciplined control again. I found a quiet, shaded corner, and sitting on the ground with my back against a pillar, I closed my eyes and proceeded to interrogate myself.

Inevitably the previous day's events loomed large in my mind; but as I mulled over what it was that was really disturbing me, I was surprised to realise that it was not the public execution of one of the Nazarenes. As calmly and dispassionately as I could, I attempted to identify what had actually happened. A young man whose Greek name suggested that he might not have been a full-blooded Jew had, mistakenly or wilfully, adopted and propagated profoundly shocking heresy. For the worst sin the Law rightly prescribed the worst penalty; and this had been justly exacted. At that precise moment my introspection was broken by the sonorous blast of the ram's horn announcing the start of the evening sacrifice. I knew that animals would be killed, and their blood displayed before God to expiate the sins of the worshippers; but the fact that the same ritual had been conducted evening and morning for countless days beforehand, and would be repeated again tomorrow and tomorrow and tomorrow, suggested that the efficacy of the act must be extremely short-lived. Was it even possible that there was no moral effectiveness in it at all? But then if that was actually the case, how could guilt be dealt with, and God's justice honoured? Yesterday's stark images forced themselves into my mind again. Again I asked myself, what was the reality behind the fleeting and fading phenomena? A man had sinned; and although his sin was outrageous, the degree of his sinfulness was almost irrelevant – it must be expunged from the sight of All-Holy God. And this could only be achieved by the sacrifice of life – the Law is inescapably explicit about that: 'It is the blood that makes atonement for one's life.' So Stephen had been rightly executed – his sin had been removed by the spilling of his blood.

But I found I could not leave it at that. My mind raced on with inexorable logic. Animal sacrifices seemed to achieve nothing. Stephen's death must surely atone for his own guilt – could this account for the serene confidence of his last words, "Lord Jesus, receive my spirit"? But where did that leave me, and my persistent awareness of my own sin? I had succeeded in repressing the thought during the weeks and months I had spent in Jerusalem – the heady excitement of new faces and new places had crowded it out of my consciousness; but now, with implacable inevitability, it surfaced to haunt me. If my reasoning so far had been correct, the only way I could clear my own guilt and justify myself before God, would be to die – and to do so voluntarily. The Scriptures teach that physical death is the inescapable consequence of sin, and I must experience it whether I want to or not. So effective expiation of my guilt demands the free and willing offering of my life. But how should I do this? Should I climb to the highest point of the Temple and throw myself down to the ground far below? It did not seem to be a particularly meaningful gesture. Should I deliberately clamber onto one of the piles of stinking refuse always smouldering in the valley of Hinnom just outside the city walls, and there immolate myself by slow incineration?

The haunting hoot of an owl snapped my reverie. This of course was ridiculous. I was letting intellectual speculation outrun common sense. There was an answer to my self-generated dilemma, and a down to earth practical one at that. I recalled my own phrase of a few moments previously – "the free and willing offering of my life". I resolved there and then to present to God the positive gift of my life, rather than its negative extinction in death – I would be useful to God, and earn his forgiveness, and justify myself by redoubling my already strenuous efforts to observe meticulously every last letter of the Law. I would do more – I would go beyond what was ordained. I was even tempted to wonder whether it would be possible to put God in my debt by doing more than he required – but I quickly dismissed the thought as blasphemous.

With a sudden surge of excitement, I realised that the means was right at hand. What could be more honouring to God than to extirpate completely the hideous heresy which Stephen had advocated? I stood up. It was nearly dark now, so I made my way back to my lodgings. My landlady managed to convey an impression of disapproval when I brushed aside the cooked meal she had prepared for me; but I was too exhilarated to eat – or to sleep, for that matter. I had a second bad night in terms of sleep. I was totally absorbed in working out in my mind the details of a campaign against the Nazarenes, or followers of the Way, or whatever other description the poor deluded disciples of Jesus might try to hide behind. I waited impatiently for cock-crow, and was outside the High Priest's house before his servant had drawn back the bars on the great wooden doors closing off the courtyard from the street. I had to wait again for an audience; but when he finally received me, the High Priest listened intently to my request for a roving commission to search these people out and punish them for their abominable apostasy. He withdrew for a while to consult with his fellow religious leaders; but eventually an attendant arrived, and with a slight bow he handed me a sealed document, with the words, "Your request is granted."

The next weeks were a flurry of activity. The High Priest had granted me wider powers than I had thought possible, including command of a posse of Temple police, mounted and armed. I had no difficulty in identifying and locating followers of this so-called 'Way'; as soon as word spread of my official appointment, informers seemed only too ready to proffer the details I needed, and I lost no time in acting on what they revealed. I swaggered ostentatiously into Solomon's Colonnade, and disposed my men in a menacing semicircle round the surprisingly large crowd of Nazarenes and their sympathisers. I had assumed that a show of force in this way would intimidate them into dispersing, and inhibit them from reassembling; but to my annoyance, I was badly mistaken. The people we were surrounding steadfastly refused to move; instead, in no time at all we were ourselves surrounded by a much larger crowd of people who left us in no doubt whatsoever as to their hostility towards us. Angry shouts and raised fists generated an atmosphere of rapidly-developing tension; I was surprised by the strength of my own feeling of relief when we eventually succeeded in extricating ourselves from what was very little short of an ugly confrontation – though I noticed that the Nazarenes themselves remained still and quiet throughout the whole episode. A change of tactics was obviously called for; if these people could attract spontaneous support on the scale we had just witnessed, a riot might easily erupt, and I could well lose the authority I had only just acquired. So we moved our operations to the night-time, and took to raiding the houses of known Nazarenes under cover of darkness. Now we met with almost no opposition, presumably because the element of surprise was on our side; in any case, a few 'accidental' deaths would, I imagined, have a salutary effect on the rest of the group.

First results of this push against the Nazarenes appeared to be encouraging. The group which had been so conspicuous in the Temple courts melted away like snow in spring-time, and I admit I preened myself on my apparent success. But I soon sensed an undercurrent of discontent in the men of my troop. I assumed it arose from boredom after the excitement of the first rush of activity; but it was not long before one of them asked if he could speak to me. "It's like this, sir", he said. "We haven't eliminated these people at all – we've merely frightened them away. They're not troubling Jerusalem any more, but me and my mates have heard them say they're popping up in all sorts of places round about. They've turned up in towns and villages all through Judaea, and in Samaria as well. There's even some that have got as far as Damascus. It's like stamping on a camp fire last thing at night, sir", he went on. "We think we've put it out, but all we've succeeded in doing is spreading sparks all around, and starting lots of little fires, and together they add up to more than the one we've extinguished." I was struck by his illustration; but I also realised that if I did not maintain the momentum of my campaign, the name I was beginning to make for myself in influential circles in Jerusalem might begin to fade from people's minds. So I sought a second audience with the High Priest, and pointing to my undeniable success in crushing the Nazarene movement in the city itself, I had no difficulty in securing an extension of my authority to arrest followers of the Way wherever I might find them, beyond, as well as within, the bounds of Judaea.

News of my extended commission had an immediate effect on my men. Fired with the prospect of renewed action, they almost outstripped me in their eagerness to be up and away. As we were still in operational mode, preparation for an extended expedition took up minimal time; and less than forty-eight hours later we were clattering out of the Damascus Gate, scattering peasants and their donkeys without concern as we headed north. We left at first light. Travelling conditions were good, and anticipation of excitement carried us all forward. We took a break during the midday heat, and had covered well over half the distance to Damascus by the time we bivouacked for the night. I was up first next morning. The day was perfect. The giant red ball of sunrise seemed to shrink as it gained in height and strengthened in brilliance in the cloudless blue sky; and heat built rapidly. The men were a little less enthusiastic about getting going – the previous day's hard riding had left us all saddle-sore and aching; but I was determined to get to Damascus before anyone could sabotage my mission by forewarning the Nazarenes there of our coming. We drove doggedly on, leaving the hot and steamy valley of the Jordan, and climbing laboriously to the hills of Galilee and Lebanon. Perversely, the heat seemed to increase with altitude. The sun beat down on us with merciless ferocity, and the men soon began to talk among themselves about a stop for rest and refreshment. I ignored them – the nearer we drew to Damascus, the more intent I became on getting there before nightfall. I had led the troop all the way; but now the sergeant spurred his mount to catch up with me. Respectfully but unmistakably, he warned me that I might have a mutiny on my hands if I did not relent and order a halt. I responded with never a word. I merely whipped my horse to even greater effort; and I allowed myself a little smile of grim satisfaction when I heard the thunder of hooves behind me continuing unabated.

The sun glared relentlessly down. I snatched a fleeting glance at it. It was a disc of burnished bronze. It occurred to me that at that time of day I ought not to be able to see it at all, for sheer brightness. I wondered if we were about to be enveloped in a sandstorm blowing in from the desert; but the light-level was not in the least diminished – in fact, I realised to my surprise that it was increasing. From the brittle brilliance refracted from sunbaked soil and heat-hardened rock, the light was changing to an absolute whiteness, so pure and intense that my eyeballs ached. I pulled my head-dress over my face. That had no effect at all. I covered my face with both hands. That made not the slightest difference – the light probed and pierced and penetrated until it seemed to separate the very bones of my body from their marrow, and my whole being felt disembowelled, naked and open to its irresistible gaze.

With both my hands off the bridle, my horse slowed from gallop to canter to trot, and then to a halt. The men behind me instinctively reined in their mounts too, and there descended a silence as searching as the light was searing. Utterly overwhelmed, I gradually realised that I was in the presence of Holiness. All that had previously gone to make me Saul – Saul from Tarsus in Cilicia, circumcised on the eighth day, of the People of Israel, of the Tribe of Benjamin, a Hebrew of Hebrews, in regard to the Law a Pharisee, as for zeal, persecuting the heretics, as for legalistic righteousness, faultless – all this lay shattered in pieces; but I lay in peace. For stupefied by light and stunned by silence, I had fallen from my horse and was now flat on the ground, face down, as one dead. And then words came, clear as the sound of a mountain stream in the time of melting snow, close at hand, but yet invisible – heartbreaking in their poignancy, devastating in their perceptiveness: "Saul, Saul, why do you persecute me?" I heard a startled reaction from my men – a sudden burst of exclaiming and questioning, instantly subsiding in bafflement and fear; but I could see nothing because of hot, inexplicable tears stinging my eyes. There was timelessness. Recognition and remorse, repentance and relationship, all resonated in the atmosphere like the after-hum of bells still thrilling the air when they have ceased sounding. At last I was brought to the point of re-birth. I heard myself quietly both asking and answering my own question – "Who are you – Lord?" "I am Jesus," he replied.

I do not know how long I lay prone; but with a sudden burst of concerned comment, my fellow riders lifted me to my feet – and then I discovered that the extremity of brilliance which had so completely dazzled me had passed into its opposite of impenetrable darkness. I could see nothing. I was hoisted onto my horse; and in sardonic mockery of my arrogant departure from Jerusalem, I was led into Damascus by a trooper walking at my horse's head, with the others doing their best to parry surprised questions and jeering comments from idle bystanders.

I learnt later that I spent three days in total trauma. My only recollection is of sitting bolt upright, with every normal function in a state of suspension. The first indication I can remember that I was still alive was the return of sound. I became aware of voices, a woman's noisily protesting, and a man's quietly insisting. The noisy one subsided, and the quiet one was suddenly right beside me. "Brother Saul," he began – and I was instantly jolted into full consciousness. I felt his hands resting lightly on my head, and I heard him refer to Jesus as Lord. Then it dawned on me that I was aware of his sleeve falling away from my face as he lowered his arms; and beyond his sleeve was his tunic, and beyond his tunic a roomful of anxious faces peering intently at me – and I was catapulted into days of suspicion and tension, of support and hostility, of bewilderment and encouragement. Weakened by the draining experience I had just been through, I sat inactive for some days at the centre of a confusing welter of advice and criticism, counsel and exhortation. I listened, and said nothing; but I took in all I heard, and weighed each comment against all the others – and above all, I prayed. Then, quite suddenly, everything fell into place. I got up one morning and calmly asked to be baptised into the Way. This one simple request dramatically polarised the contentions and contradictions still surging all round me. One group pointedly commented that I had come to Damascus with authority from the chief priests to arrest all who call on the Name of Jesus, and that I should be shunned as an obvious would-be infiltrator; but a larger number agreed to my request, and after I had made convincing answers to searching questions, water was sprinkled over me in a simple ceremony, and I was acknowledged as a follower of the Way.

The effect of baptism on me was immediate and dramatic. The very next Sabbath I asked for permission to speak in the synagogue, and – I know not how – words poured out of me, proclaiming Jesus as the Child of God. All I knew was that I had been through deep, deep darkness, and had come out on the other side into pure and perfect light. A huge obstacle had been jamming the stream of my life; now it was gone, and everything now made sense as my gifts, my training, my experience, combined in one unhindered flow. I knew now, in a way I had never known before, the point and purpose of life; I experienced a primal surge of fulfilment as I realised that I had been created and chosen for the one supreme task of carrying the Name of Jesus before the people of Israel – and perhaps, I fleetingly dreamt, even before Gentiles and their kings.

The only trouble was that scarcely anybody else seemed to see it that way. I suppose I should hardly have been surprised. My fame had gone before me as the man who had caused havoc in Jerusalem among the people who called on the Name, and who had come to Damascus to take Nazarenes there as prisoners to the chief priests. I faced a huge challenge in turning this perception round;

but I was profoundly grateful for the thorough grounding I had received in the Scriptures – passage after passage came to my mind to use in discussions and debates with the Jews of Damascus, to demonstrate how Jesus of Nazareth perfectly fulfilled all the Fathers' expectations of the Messiah who was to come. As a result, it was not only perceptions that turned round; relationships were also rapidly reversed. The people who had trembled at my coming slowly but surely became my most stout-hearted supporters, while those who had gleefully looked forward to my arrival very quickly turned to angry hostility. Those were testing days. I had been through an experience so profound, so totally penetrating, that it had completely remade me. All my previous assumptions and attitudes and values had been stood on their head. I slowly came to realise that I had not merely been transformed; I had been made anew, so completely and comprehensively that I was no longer who I had been. It was as if I had been born again – I was an entirely new creature, solely through the grace, the undeserved kindness, of God. The fact was so overwhelming in its reality that I felt I had to give unmistakable expression to it; so I began to let it be known that I would in future like to be known as Paul – I am after all far from being the tallest of men! But of course that was immediately interpreted as being at the very least devious, but much more likely, cowardly – I was accused of trying to evade the consequences of my change of heart by disowning my entire previous existence. In my heart of hearts I knew that there was a sense in which this did not go even part of the way towards explaining what had happened to me. I was not disowning my previous existence – I had finished with it, completed it, closed the last chapter of it. I had actually died to it – in the profoundest sense possible, my death was now behind me. But I accepted that all this would be utterly baffling to anyone who had not experienced it; indeed, though vividly real and undeniable, it was still quite inexplicable to me. I was still fired by the afterglow of my encounter with the Living Jesus; I had not had time to reflect on it, analyse it, think through any of the implications of it, or work out the practical consequences of it.

Neither did I have the opportunity to do so. I was not merely in the thick of controversy – I was at the very centre of it. I had no option but to accept every invitation, to seize every opportunity – or to create one if none offered itself – of proclaiming Jesus as Lord. Nor was this limited to the set hours for worship in the synagogue. My fellow-believers and I set the whole Jewish community in Damascus by the ears with our preaching; and argument and hostility, debate and controversy, circled round us continuously, day and night. My theological training had been theoretical only, with virtually no practical content – I was not prepared for the hurly-burly of confrontation in the synagogue and the market-place, on the street, and even at my lodgings; and I soon began to feel the strain. I was physically stressed and emotionally drained. Though I was often utterly exhausted, I suffered sleepless nights. My mind would not rest, and my body could not relax; my limbs twitched uncontrollably, and painful cramps increasingly tormented my toes and calves and thighs. Headaches developed, and steadily became more frequent and more intense. I began to suffer split vision. Half of what I saw was quite normal, but the rest was a mix of painfully bright stars and circles endlessly moving and changing their shapes, and lightning-like flashes of light seeming to stab to the very centre of my eyeballs. I felt nauseous and sick. I retched and retched but could not vomit. I was totally incapacitated by these attacks. I had no choice but to lie on my mat in a darkened room, and wait with increasing desperation for sleep. Conditioned by the habit of a lifetime, I turned to

God in prayer; but no answer came, until at last, after I know not how many hours or even days of unassuaged pain, my body could take no more, and I sank into fitful slumber.

When I eventually woke, my head still throbbed, as if it had been trampled on by a herd of racing camels; but the vicious piercing pain had ceased, and I was able to sit up and begin to take food and drink again. But I quickly gathered that my indisposition had been seized upon by my opponents as proof that both I and the message I proclaimed were of the Devil. Even some of the Nazarenes were uneasy about me now. "Surely," they whispered among themselves, "if the Lord was with this man he would not let him have suffered in this way. He is possessed by demons, not by the Holy Spirit." My heart sank as I took in the implication of this. It seemed that despite all my efforts, and contrary to all my intentions, I had actually become an embarrassment to the believers in Damascus, and a hindrance to their determination to spread the Good News. I reflected bitterly that the most effective way of helping them in this appeared to be to remove myself from them altogether. Weakened by the succession of harrowing experiences I had been through since I left Jerusalem, I succumbed to depression. The first burst of my enthusiasm evaporated. I felt I was not up to the demands of the calling I had so recently been so sure of. I needed time and space to wind down, and in cool detachment to take apart everything that had happened to me, examine it dispassionately, assess it rationally – and then, if it still stood up to the most rigorous evaluation I could bring to it, to put it all together again on a solid basis, probed and proven and unshakeable. Having identified my goal, I braced myself to will the means to the end. I waited for the next moonless night and then, without a word to anybody, I slipped out of the house I had been staying in and moved watchfully through the silent streets. My spirits lifted when I reached the city wall; the main gate was of course closed, but there was no sign of a guard on duty at the little 'eye of the needle' beside it. I took it as some kind of vindication of my decision when I passed through the low, man-sized aperture, and was able to reach the shelter of palm-trees beyond the open space outside without encountering a single human being, or having to parry any challenge or question. A sleepy protest from a disturbed bird was the only impact I made when I left the city of Damascus for the solitude of the desert.

IV

SUBORDINATION

ARABIA is different. Arabia is different from anything else I have ever encountered. Arabia is desert. But Arabia is not deserted. Travelling on foot, I struck out east from Damascus. In the absence of stimuli to my other senses, my footfalls at first seemed startlingly loud as my sandals slapped on hard rock, or shuffled through sifting sand; but the blackness of the night reluctantly relented, and allowed the light of the coming day to soften its hard edge. Behind me the mountains of Lebanon caught and held the first rays of the rising sun, their peaks a different hue each time I turned to look at them; while in front of me the desert plain stretched far away beyond the limits of my vision. But it was an untidy scene. Unrelated outcrops of rock lay about, as if scattered at random by some careless giant hand. Here and there were occasional isolated stands of palm trees, small, stunted, sad-looking – there was no fruit on them when I would have dearly loved to gather some as the day wore on, and I grew weary with my journey. But everywhere there was sand – sand underfoot, sand whirling in little eddies in the air as a breeze stirred it up, sand in my clothes and hair and beard, sand irritating my eyes, sand stinging my face as the wind strengthened, and then sand obliterating the landscape behind light brown clouds as it drifted aimlessly at the mercy of capricious air currents. Occasionally there were people. At first light I saw a shepherd leading his flock in search of sparse grass; and a little later I heard the haunting notes of a small pipe, as a boy tending goats both amused himself and gave his charges a point of reference, lest they strayed too far for him to keep track of them. Farther off, a camel-train made an intriguing silhouette against an unvarying backdrop of sand dunes as it swayed slowly away in the distance; it finally disappeared – and I realised that I was now entirely alone. I felt a slight twinge of fear. This was irrational – I had deliberately sought the solitude of the desert, believing that it would give me an opportunity to reintegrate my near-shattered self-perception; but I had lived in town or city all my life, and I was wholly unprepared for the stark contrast between the imagined idyll and the rude reality. I realised that, scant though they were, I had held on to each sighting of other human beings with an unconsciously intense gratitude – they represented support, security, reassurance; but now they were gone, and for the first time in my life I was thrown back on myself, and my own resourcefulness. Then that word sparked other associations, and my mood changed, even though only slightly. I reminded myself that I was a fully-grown human being, on the threshold of adult maturity, with physical and mental powers all unimpaired; but even as I felt a ripple of pride course through my self awareness, my self-generated confidence began to crumble. I was unnerved by the vastness of the empty desert all around me, in some strange way intimidated by the hugeness of the implacable hot blue sky overhead, unreasonably threatened by the cold indifference of the whole of nature to me, and my needs, and my dilemma. But then my upbringing and training asserted themselves as another line of thought presented itself to me. I was a child of

Abraham, a member of God's Chosen People, a son of the Law – and now, I was beginning to understand, even more than that; much, much more than that. I had seen Jesus of Nazareth, alive, with unmistakable nail marks on his hands, and the scars of thorn prickles on his forehead, and yet radiating a vibrant unearthly glory. He had challenged me by name, and I had been completely subdued by Him. I could not deny that – nor could I ever go back on it. I had deliberately sought the loneliness of the desert in order to begin to come to terms with what had happened – I had almost unthinkingly assumed that freedom from every kind of distraction would serve to concentrate my mind on spiritual matters, and sharpen my awareness of the presence of God. But perhaps I had rushed into it too precipitately – with the brash impatience of youth I had failed to appreciate the need to school myself to the demands and effects of solitude and silence, fasting and rootlessness. I vaguely wondered whether my vacillating mental states were the first results of going without food; but I knew that I was not experiencing light-headedness. In fact, as the light began to fade, my mind focused more sharply on the desirability of finding some sort of shelter – I knew that nights in the desert are as cold as the days are hot. A distant dark green smudge on the all-enveloping sea of brown beckoned irresistibly; and my first night away from the trappings of civilisation was spent under the shelter of protective palm trees, with the soothing sound of gently-running water to lull me into grateful sleep.

I was surprised by the ease with which I slipped into a routine relevant to my new environment. True, I woke each morning stiff and cold, still unaccustomed to the rigours of sleeping under the stars; but my body rapidly adjusted to a new regime of light diet and long days of walking and meditation. For I found that after initial disappointments, the benefits I had originally hoped for began to materialise. The preoccupations of town life steadily faded from my mind, and every aspect of my consciousness increasingly centred on God. It was not that I made a determined, sustained effort to swing my thoughts in that particular direction; rather, I became aware that I was being drawn into an ever-closer and ever-deepening awareness of God. The prophet Jeremiah's parable of clay being moulded by the potter came dramatically alive for me; but at the same time I passed beyond it, for I knew that I was very far from being merely inert material in the hands of an uncommunicative manipulator. I was given an altogether new experience; I entered into a living relationship with a real person – Jesus, God's Chosen One. I turned over and over in my mind the insights shared with me by the believers in Damascus; and in prayer and contemplation I explored their depths, scaled their heights, and made them mine. In depressing remorse I recalled the grace and power of Stephen's proclamation of Jesus in Jerusalem; and tears filled my eyes as I recalled the patience with which he had endured the blatant bias of his trial by the Sanhedrin, and the serenity he had displayed when his tormentors – when we – triumphantly hemmed him in, and savagely sated on him our primitive lust for blood. I was crushed beyond comforting by the inescapable realisation that he had been right, and that I, as bitterly opposed as I had been to everything he said, and stood for, and died for, had been wrong. I cried out loud in the deaf desert for God to forgive me; and in the silence of the ensuing nights and days there slowly grew within me – no, there steadily entered me from outside, from above – the understanding that in his Child, Jesus, God had effectively dealt with my guilt, by atoning for my wilful wickedness in taking on Himself the punishment due for my sin, and restoring to me that holiness without which no one can see Him. I was granted the conviction, at once both deeply humbling, and gloriously liberating, that God had fully answered Stephen's last gasped prayer – "Lord, do not hold this sin against them." As this almost unbelievable truth spread its life-restoring light throughout my entire being, my spirit leapt and soared and sang. I was free – morally, spiritually, really, free; not because I had escaped my deserts – I was still devastated by the memory of violence and murder – but because they had been lifted from me: and lifted from me, not by a weak, indulgent Parent glossing over the abhorrent evil of sin and debasing the worth of mercy, but lifted from me by the One and Only Holy God Himself descending to the depths of my depravity, drinking my bitter degradation to the very dregs, and offering me as an undeserved gift, free forgiveness, release from guilt, and a restoration of that relationship with Himself for which I had been created, and which I had ruptured by my own wretched, reckless wrongdoing.

My reaction as all this understanding flooded over me could not be expressed in mere words. I stood with arms upraised and head thrown back to express, in sounds beyond the rationality of language, praise and gratitude that not only had God done all this, but that he had chosen to open my blind eyes to see what he had done, to enlighten my dark mind to understand what he had done, and to move my stubborn will to accept what he had done. I knelt in fervent adoration of the inconceivable love which had condescended to do all this for me. I prostrated myself in the sand of the desert and poured out worship in mute ecstasy.
And then the Spirit came.

There was movement far away. The horizon became obscured as a cloud of sand blurred the distinction between earth and sky. A sudden breeze moved the hem of my cloak and the edges of my sleeves. The cloud moved towards me across the desert, and the breeze stiffened. A low humming sound reached my ears, and the light noticeably brightened. The strength of the wind steadily increased, and the palm trees leaned away from it, as if in awe of it. The cloud advanced rapidly towards me, changing as it did from yellow-brown to radiant gold, and the sound accompanying it separated out into rumbles of thunder, fanfares as from trumpets, the jubilant clashing of a myriad of cymbals, and the thrilling pealing of innumerable bells. Lightning flashed all round, vivid but unthreatening, ethereal colours glowed everywhere, constantly moving and melding, and I was lifted up as in a chariot of pure fire. I was totally enveloped in glory, glory such as could emanate only from God. Transports of joy flooded my whole being, and spiritual rapture searched into every remotest corner of my consciousness, sweeping clean away all my self disgust, my doubt, my preoccupation with the physical world, my obsession with material things. I was raised to the realms of reality, I heard truths human ears can scarcely bear; and I saw again the Living Jesus Who had first won my allegiance on the road to Damascus.

I do not know how long I was out of the body, in the Spirit; but afterwards a great calm descended upon me. I knew serenity of soul and tranquillity of mind. I felt utterly fulfilled – at one with nature, at ease with myself, at peace with God. My thoughts turned eagerly to the records in the Scriptures of the experiences of others who had been granted the vision of God. I warmed to the response of Jacob and the reaction of Moses, I understood Isaiah's worship and Ezekiel's wonder – above all, I now knew what Stephen had experienced. A lump came to my throat as I reflected on how grossly I had misunderstood him, but how gloriously faithful he had been to the Risen Lord, even unto death. I shuddered as the recollection of my part in that seeped again into my mind; and I turned to God with a strong prayer that if I should ever be brought into the situation he faced, I might remain as steadfast to the end as he had been.

Once again, I had found myself swept into fathomless depths of experience which had totally remade me; and once again I knew I needed time and space to absorb and assimilate what had happened to me, and to come to terms with so many new life-changing challenges. So I was grateful for the desert, and the opportunity it afforded of reflecting, and reasoning, and resolving. I was less restless now, and spent more time in and around the welcome oases, savouring the scents of aromatic plants, watching the fascinating but elusive ostriches, sharing noontide shade with camels, and night time shelter with the occasional horse, or even an adventurous wild ass. I gained some respect from proud and fiercely independent Bedouin tribesmen by demonstrating technical expertise with tent construction and repairs. They rewarded me by drawing me into the circle round evening camp fires. I heard fascinating tales of their travels to far-distant lands to trade the spices of the desert for the silks of the Orient. Sometimes there was talk of gold and precious stones to be mined from the earth – perhaps beneath the very sites of the camps we were occupying; but nobody knew for sure, and it was too remote a chance for anyone to invest the time and energy required for the effort to prove worthwhile. I spent just about all of my time and energy in thought and prayer, until eventually it became clear to me that the time for withdrawal from the world had come to an end, and that I must now take up the task for which I had been so unexpectedly prepared. So I returned to Damascus.

Immediately I was back in the thick of things. It proved wise to have left the believers for a while, not only for my own sake, but for theirs as well. During my absence they had obviously debated among themselves the genuineness of my conversion, for when I arrived back in the city they welcomed me with transparent sincerity; and in no time at all I found myself heading up the proclamation of the Good News of Jesus whenever opportunities presented themselves. It was fascinating to observe reactions to the message; there were always three distinct groups – those who publicly aligned themselves with us, those who vigorously opposed us, and the majority, who listened and watched, usually with great interest, but showed no sign of committing themselves either way. I was struck by the fact that the first two groups were virtually always fellow Jews; the third were largely Gentiles. I fell to wondering whether God's saving acts were effective only for his Chosen People; but the question only served to lead on to a further question – could it possibly be that the term 'Chosen People' was about to be redefined? Were they now to be identified by a characteristic other than racial origin? My training had made me aware of a number of hints in the Scriptures that God's salvation might eventually encompass the whole human race, not just the descendants of Abraham – but the pressures of daily controversy promptly pushed this speculation to the back of my mind. It didn't go away altogether, however – partly, I suspect, because of the virulent hostility displayed by the most orthodox members of the synagogue in Damascus. As a Pharisee myself I was well equipped to dispute with them – I knew their position from the inside, and quickly realised that I was ideally suited to answer their objections to the proclamation that Jesus of Nazareth was indeed the long awaited and imminently expected Messiah.

Eventually they betrayed their awareness that my familiarity with their beliefs marked me out as their most dangerous opponent. It must have been getting on for three years after I returned to Damascus that I began to suspect that I was being spied upon. At first I lightly dismissed the thought as a superficial neurosis – more than likely I had developed some lopsided thinking as a result of those weeks in the desert, suddenly deprived without preparation of the wholesome counterbalance of other people's opinions and reactions, and probably exposed without protection to too much sun and wind. But the suspicion persisted. I had an uneasy sense that there was often a sinister presence not far away, even when I was lost in the anonymity of the crowds thronging the city's streets. There was of course an easy way of confirming or refuting my fears. I approached a friendly young fellow believer, who willingly agreed to tail me at a distance whenever I went out – he clearly relished the prospect of intrigue and adventure opening out before him. Less than a week after he agreed to do this, he knocked at the door of my lodgings. I let him in. I noticed that he glanced quickly around him as he entered. "Are we alone, sir?" he asked quietly. "Yes, of course we are", I grinned back. "Why? – have you discovered anything?" He nodded slowly, and then began to tell me that he had indeed discovered that I was being followed. "There is a small swarthy man who always seems to be on the same street as you are, and to take the same route as you do, whichever way you go. It's easy for me to follow him – he always wears the same clothes! I think it's highly suspicious", my young friend earnestly informed me. "You should go out as little as possible," he went on, "but when you have to, never go at the same time of day, and always go a different way", he helpfully advised me. I thanked him for his assistance, and decided on reflection to take a few of my most trusted acquaintances into my confidence. Between them they constituted an effective local network, with numbers of useful contacts in different spheres of the city's life; and it was not long before they came to me with some very unsettling intelligence. "There is a contract out on your life," one of them grimly informed me, "and we suspect we have learnt of it only just in time. They plan to kidnap you off the street the very next time you set foot outside the door – you could be dead by this time tomorrow." The seriousness in the speaker's voice shattered my last vestiges of complacency. "We've got to get you out of Damascus tonight!" he emphasised. "Fat chance of that", interjected a burly straight-speaking local man. "We've discovered they've got armed men at each of the city gates, twenty-four hours a day." A quietly spoken older man said, "I think there's a possible way round that. I know a man whose house backs right on to the city wall – he actually has a window in the wall itself. It's big enough for you to squeeze through – you're not a big chap, are you?" he commented, eyeing me up and down for all the world as if I was livestock he was thinking of buying. "That looks like your best chance," someone else remarked, "maybe your only chance." Suddenly I found myself taken over. "Right, we'll get this organised for tonight. You, alert your house-on-the-wall-owning friend – you, find a man-sized basket in the market – you, get a coil of rope long enough to reach the ground and strong enough to hold him up, and you," – this directed to me – "be ready to leave here at sunset." The group left the house at staggered intervals, and I followed last of all, with the young man who had confirmed my first suspicions as my guide. "Pull your shawl well round your face", he told me. He did the same, and looked carefully up and down the street before letting me out of the door.

It was immediately obvious that he knew Damascus like the back of his hand. He took me down alleyways I had never seen before, across courtyards I swear I could never find again if I had to, and finally up a long flight of steps to a raised walkway providing access to a row of houses backing onto the city wall. He hurried me to a door and bundled me unceremoniously inside as soon as it was opened. I recognised the people who had gathered at my lodgings earlier in the day. "Now the first thing you'll need is a good meal inside you", one of them said; but despite the delicious smell of cooking coming from the pot on the fire, I contradicted him. "No," I said, "the first thing we all need is the assurance of the presence of God." So, with the comforting sound of a hot stew gently plopping and bubbling as background, we stood in a circle and prayed for each other. Then it was time to eat the evening meal together. By the time we had finished it was completely dark outside. Mercifully, it was a moonless night. The basket with the rope attached was in place. I climbed up to the opening in the wall of the room we were in and, pushing the basket in front of me, I crawled along the short tunnel towards the rectangle of stars at the end of it — only to find that I had to back all the way into the room again, because there wasn't enough space for me to turn round in the tunnel. It was only a minor setback, but it unnerved me. A wave of apprehension swept over me; but things had now gone too far to allow of any turning back. "Here, I almost forgot to give you this", whispered the householder's wife, as she pressed a small food pack into my hand. "Tuck it into your belt — it'll help to keep you going for the next few hours." I wasn't sure whether I detected a break in her voice as she spoke; but I had no time to wonder. I crawled backwards through the tunnel, clutching the rope held by the men in the room. I lowered myself gingerly over the edge and into the basket. I had to look down; but there was neither sight nor sound of any kind of movement. I looked up at the parapet above me; there was no sign of life or activity there, either. I nodded to the man at the front of the rope, and as he passed the word back I felt myself being let down as the rope was slowly handed out. The basket swayed and wobbled more than I had expected it to, and the sound of it knocking and scraping against the massive stone wall seemed alarmingly loud. There was an oddly reassuring bump as it grounded – but then it tipped over onto its side, and I had to crawl out between the lifting ropes. I gave one sharp tug on the main rope, and watched anxiously as the basket was hauled back up to the window in the wall. As soon as it was safely inside, I turned to move away – and instantly froze in terror. In the deep silence of the night I detected the unmistakable sound of horses' hooves, far away at first, but steadily drawing nearer. I looked round frantically. There was a small hollow in the ground beside me, right where the wall rose up into the night sky. I flung myself into it and lay face down, trembling uncontrollably. The sound of horses trotting came inexorably on. My heart was pounding with fear – this must be the military. In the long drawn out seconds that followed I marvelled at the timing which had allowed the basket to disappear from the wall, but had prevented me from breaking cover and moving directly into danger. Then they were upon me. They were indeed cavalry – not Roman cavalry, but men in the uniforms of Aretas IV, the Nabatacan king whose Governor controlled the city of Damascus, and whose men were the very people with instructions to arrest me. I flattened myself again into the ground, against the reassuring protection of the wall, not even daring to breathe – and then they were gone, riding on unconcerned into the night; I even heard a snatch of relaxed conversation between two of them as they passed within feet of where I was lying. It took me what seemed like ages to muster sufficient courage to lift my head and look around again – I was afraid of mistaking the pounding of my heart for the thud of another detachment of mounted troops; but eventually I risked standing up, and finally took a few faltering steps away from the blackness of the wall, into the blue of the night. I reflected ruefully that this was the second time I had left Damascus surreptitiously, under cover of darkness. It all seemed a bit undignified for a proud member of the most exclusive sect within Judaism – would following Jesus consign me permanently to an underprivileged minority, subject now to just the same virulent persecution as I had earlier unleashed on them myself? Would I always be hunted and hounded from pillar to post, a refugee, an exile, in effect a wanted criminal with a price on my head? These were the gloomy thoughts that persistently presented themselves to me as I strode through the night, anxious to put as great a distance as possible between me and the city of Damascus, in the shortest possible time. I walked until exhaustion overwhelmed me; then I curled up gratefully in the shelter of a cleft in the rocks on my left. Sleep was virtually instantaneous; but in the last seconds of consciousness I suddenly saw, as clearly as when it first happened, the face of Ananias, the man who, when I was led blind into Damascus, had laid his hands on me in healing, and I heard him tell me again what he had been told by the Lord Jesus – "I will show him how much he must suffer for my Name."

V
DEJECTION

SO I came again to Jerusalem, a good three years or more after I had left it so cockily – and my second entry was as inauspicious as my first had been. Once again I found myself unavoidably sucked into the vortex of people funnelled by the need to pass through the narrow city gate; and I was as indiscriminately pummelled and jostled as I had been on the previous occasion. Then I had been a complete stranger to everybody, known to none, ignored by all; now I was a marked man, wanted for treachery by the authorities, suspected of duplicity by the people I needed to help me. I sighed heavily to myself as the remembered sights of the city forced these facts into my mind; but my immediate goal was to establish contact with the followers of the Way in Jerusalem, and convince them of the genuineness of my conversion.

I was surprised by the huge effort I had to make to do this. All my natural pride rose up in rebellion against the humiliation of having to seek out ordinary working people, and plead with them to accept me as one of themselves; and I discovered that my reluctance to approach them was, not surprisingly, fully matched by their reluctance to accept me. Then my dilemma was resolved in a way which seemed to me as miraculous as the deliverance of the people trapped between the Reed Sea and the forces of Pharaoh, on their way from Egypt to the Promised Land. I became aware of a man standing beside one of the stalls in a small market-square in the city. He was staring hard at me, and as his gaze caught mine, we recognised each other simultaneously. "Junias!" I exclaimed, at the same moment as he said, "Saul!" "No," I said with a gentle smile, "you have always known me as Saul – but now I am Paul." "Why?" he asked. "Because" – and here I took a very deep breath indeed – "I am a completely new person." His eyes noticeably narrowed. "What do you mean – a new person? Are you fleeing from the law, or something?" "No," I slowly responded. "In ultimate terms I have been freed from the Law. I have become a follower of Jesus of Nazareth." Junias' eyes became as wide as they had just been narrow, and his mouth opened and closed more than once as he fought for words to utter. I braced myself for what I assumed would be a torrent of savage abuse. Finally he managed to splutter, "What? You, my own first cousin – a fellow believer?" Now it was my turn to be momentarily paralysed. "Why," I eventually squeaked, "are you one also?" By now the stall-holder was eyeing us both with very much more than casual interest. Following my apprehensive glance, Junias quickly reassured me. "Oh, don't be alarmed," he said; "he's a fellow believer too." But I immediately sensed that the stall-holder felt he had every reason to be alarmed; as Junias and I moved away in eager conversation, I could see out of the corner of my eye animated gestures and agitated expressions which could mean only one thing – I was already the unintentional cause of directly opposed opinions within the nervous group. Junias and I had not met for years, but the family connection enabled him to accept without quibble my assertion of faith in Jesus as the Messiah. Understandably enough, however, the people in the fellowship who had

See Acts 15:39 ⤴

known me, or heard tell of me, as their arch persecutor, showed no such readiness to receive me on my own say so. But the God Who had opened the Reed Sea for the Fathers continued to open the way for me as well; Junias introduced me to Barnabas.

<u>Barnabas was the most constant friend I ever had.</u> He ? was one of those people who seem to have been endowed with more gifts than most. He was a big man with an ever-ready smile, and, as is often the case with big men, a most gentle spirit. His eyes twinkled ceaselessly above his bushy beard, and his booming voice was all of a piece with his hearty handshake. I later found out that he came from a wealthy family with estates on the island of Cyprus; but I was told that as soon as he joined the followers of the Way, he sold all his lands, and donated the proceeds to the common fund which had been set up for the benefit of all the believers. Nor was his generosity limited to merely material things – when Junias introduced me to him, and explained my predicament, he insisted that I should regard his home as my own. His genial, uncomplicated friendliness left no room for dissent, and I spent two very enjoyable weeks as a guest in his large and well appointed house in Jerusalem. They were busy weeks, exciting, packed with new experiences – and exhausting. Barnabas and I talked long into the night, probing each other's experience of Jesus, sharing insights, benefiting from each other's perceptions. We found we had much in common; but at the same time our individual characteristics appeared to complement each other – or so it seemed to us then, on first acquaintance. In only a matter of days it was obvious that Barnabas had concluded that I was a genuine believer, not a sort of Trojan Horse, infiltrated in order to trick all the others into betraying themselves. My acceptance was sealed when I was introduced to Peter, the leader of the believers. We had both heard of each other; now it was

fascinating to meet the man who had once been my top priority for extermination. Peter was smaller than Barnabas, stocky and sturdy, with just the physique appropriate for, and developed by, his life as a fisherman on Lake Galilee. His hands were large and rough, but his eyes, most unusually, were blue – in a fanciful moment I reflected that they echoed the blue of the lake; but I also discovered that they could change as rapidly as the water of the lake, from unruffled serenity, through restlessness, to stormy darkness. Peter's greeting was warm and unaffected; but I still sensed a guarded attitude towards me, in contrast to Barnabas' uninhibited openness. I had to remind myself again that in view of my former reputation, this was perfectly understandable; but there was something more to it than that. In unguarded moments Peter's expression sometimes seemed to betray a troubled spirit; he gave the impression that he was brooding over a sense of unworthiness, past unhappiness, failure, perhaps – but these were only fleeting occasions. When I heard him speak in Solomon's Colonnade in the Temple, I realised that he was a man transformed; he was so taken up with what he was saying – or rather, Who he was talking about – that I recognised in him what I already knew about myself. He, like me, was more than merely transformed; he was, like me, a new creation.

I listened intently, and learned a lot from Peter. I could scarcely believe that I was seeing and hearing someone who had actually lived and worked and talked with Jesus – the realisation was breathtaking, and I valued those two weeks as I have valued no others, before or since. Though he was slower to give himself than Barnabas was, he nevertheless shared with me as fully as he could, in the short time we had together, his memories of Jesus, and the impact made on him by all that he had experienced during the three years leading up to Jesus' execution. I eagerly drank in everything he was able to give, and tried to utilise to the full this priceless opportunity of making good as much as I could of my own lack of knowledge and understanding. And then I was given another unexpected privilege – I met James. Here was a man who had come to realise that Jesus is the Messiah by a very different route; he had known Jesus all his life. James is an austere man, even – sometimes – severe. He came over as something of a hard-headed realist. He freely admitted to me that growing up with Jesus had actually delayed his recognition that here, at long last, was God's Own Chosen One. That was understandable – anyone would find it hard to acknowledge that the ordinary, the everyday, the familiar, was actually shot through with all the glory and grace of the Godhead. James sighed as he related how he and his brothers and sisters had all been convinced that Jesus was suffering from megalomania; apparently, at one stage even Jesus' mother had joined them in marching off to where her son was teaching, and demanding that he stop all this nonsense forthwith, and come straight back home with them, there and then. I warmed to Peter more than to James, and to Barnabas more than to Peter; but James was as valuable to me as both of the others. He had insights into the character of Jesus which the other two, by the very nature of things, could not have. He and Peter were at that time joint leaders of the Jerusalem believers; my assessment of them was that Peter possessed a more compelling charisma, but James displayed greater practical competence. Certainly they seemed to complement each other's gifts; but I remember idly wondering whether there might at some time be tension between the two of them, and if so, which of them might emerge as the single leader of the group.

But these pleasant speculations were suddenly rudely interrupted. I experienced a sharp sense of déjà vu when one of the believers came late one night to Barnabas' house with an urgent warning that my life was in dire danger from jealous Jews. As in Damascus, so in Jerusalem – the proclamation of the Good News about Jesus sliced through the faithful like a hot knife through butter. The wonder of those chosen to believe was just about paralleled in intensity by the anger of those who were outraged by the message; and tragically, the latter were convinced, just as I had once been, that they would honour God by stamping out the very mention of the Name of Jesus. So virulent was their hatred of me in particular, that the brothers in Jerusalem acted as promptly as those in Damascus had done; before I had time to take formal leave of anyone, I found myself out of the house, in the back of a wagon, jolting uncomfortably through two nights and a day, and ending up, just as dawn was breaking, in the splendid city of Caesarea, beside the Great Sea. I was however given no time to admire its architecture, or sample its seductive sophistication – my caring friends were insistent that I should remove myself completely from any possibility of danger; and the sight of the sea generated a sudden surge of homesickness in me. I had been away from home long enough to want to go back again, to find out how everyone was, to pick up the threads of my former life, to see what had changed, and what was still the same. Resolution fed on reflection, and in less than a week I was on the move again. I stood in the prow of a medium sized coastal merchantman destined for the coast of Cilicia, and watched the gleaming white buildings of Herod the Great's sumptuous tribute to his patron, Augustus Caesar, glide slowly by, dazzlingly white against the brilliant azure of the cloudless morning sky. I realised with pleasant surprise that one gets an altogether different impression of a built-up area from the sea, or from a hill top, than from laboriously trudging its streets on foot. A friendly crewman, presumably a native of the city, pointed out its temple, its theatre, its amphitheatre, all of them built within the last fifty years at the most; they seemed positively to preen themselves on their still-pristine beauty, and to invite admiring appreciation. Then we were past the tower at the end of the long mole enclosing the huge harbour, and my informant was gone, engrossed now in his work as the waves outside the protection of the harbour slapped at the port side of the boat. We ploughed slowly north through the choppy waters of the open sea. A few of my fellow passengers soon began to look decidedly queasy; but I found to my delight that I positively enjoyed sailing. A stiff southerly blew steadily. I spent most of my time on deck, revelling in the warm kiss of the sun and the rough caress of the wind, delighted by the challenge of finding and holding my balance against the pitch and roll of the ship's deck, and ravished by the stab of nostalgia which surged over me when I heard again the cries of sea birds – a sound I had not heard since I first left Tarsus, almost four years previously. The sandy-brown coastline drifted lazily by to starboard, and for a few blessed days the rhythm of life eased into a slow, gentle swing. I gratefully filled my lungs with sea-clean dust-free air, and felt my mind relax, and let go of the preoccupations and concerns which I now perceived only served to tense and tighten it. Stress and strain ebbed away, serenity and calm flowed in their place, and I became aware of the deep peace of God, a peace past my understanding. For the first time in what seemed by contrast to have been a too highly strung life, I was able to let go of myself, and sink back into the unassailable security of total trust in God. I took to sleeping on deck – there was space below, but although it was warmer there, it was too stuffy and smelly for me. There was no shortage of thick woollen blankets, and wrapped up snugly, I lay on my back, watching the top of the mast describe a slow, repeated, hypnotic arc across the silver stars set in the dark velvet of the sky. The regular flap of the sail as it responded to the rise and fall of the wind had a curiously soporific effect on me; and the occasional sing-song call of lookout to helmsman barely intruded on my fading consciousness as I slowly drifted away into the deep of sleep.

The long lazy days were punctuated when the captain put in to various ports on our northward voyage – Ptolemais, Tyre, Sarepta, Sidon, Seleucia, among others. Then the therapy of slow sea travel was balanced by the bustle and hubbub of busy harbours. Wooden gangplanks were lashed securely to the deck railing, and the ship listed almost imperceptibly as crewmen, half naked in midday heat, toiled and sweated and cursed under huge bundles of whatever it was that needed to be unloaded on the quayside – only to be replaced by equally huge and heavy cargoes stacked at the water's edge for transit to upcoming destinations. Ropes creaked complainingly against restraining bollards, seagulls shrieked overhead, children darted excitedly in and out of little knots of traders striking deals, of customs officials exacting dues, of seamen chafing about a drop in the wind or arguing about the time of the next high tide – and then it all suddenly subsided as ropes were cast off, the sail began to belly out in the breeze, the bows ploughed a purposeful path through the water, and the stern slowly generated a white wash betraying the way we had taken. It was all immensely satisfying, and I caught myself half wishing the idyll would continue indefinitely; but the day came when the captain ordered the helmsman to take bearings, first for the west, and then for the north again, and the land began to close in on both sides as we entered the estuary of the Cydnus. I experienced strange reactions as we moved slowly up-river to Tarsus; childhood memories surfaced as we came in sight of places where I had played as a boy, or explored with friends – the scenes were the same, and yet not the same. It dawned on me that it was I who had changed – I was the cause of the unease I felt at the failure of my recollections to chime harmoniously with my experience of the present. But the familiar contours of the town struck a responsive chord in me as the captain let the ship drift slowly to bump against the stout wooden bulwarks of the quayside; and yet they were not familiar, for I had never seen my hometown from the river before. The vague sense of disenchantment deepened as I stepped ashore and walked the street to my parents' house. Nearly half a decade had passed since I first left home, and I suddenly had an unsettling feeling of being at a disadvantage; the people I passed in the street knew what had happened there in the past five years or so, and I did not. Their relationships with each other had developed, or deteriorated, and I was no longer aware of how each stood with the other. The old, comfortable, innate sense of belonging had evaporated, and I was now an outsider. I did not meet anyone I knew; but I was conscious of being stared at curiously, even suspiciously. The dreary realisation dawned on me that I was a stranger in the very place that had given me birth.

But I cheered up when I reached home. The welcome I received more than compensated for the initial disappointment I had felt at the end of my voyage; my father permitted himself a broad grin when he opened the door to my knock, and slapped me delightedly on the back, and my mother gave way to tears of joy. I felt a lump of emotion rise in my throat, and tears stung my own eyes as we held each other in a long embrace. Then there was excited babble as questions and answers tumbled over each other in our eagerness to catch up with everything that had happened while I had been away. The lamp burned long into the night, until we were abruptly interrupted when it went out – in our excitement none of us had thought to replenish the oil; so we groped our way to bed, and began next morning to stitch together a more coherent account of events and people. My father's brow furrowed, and my mother fell strangely silent, when I told them how I had become convinced that God had at long last fulfilled his ancient promise of a Deliverer for his people. "Yes," said my mother in a flat tone of voice, "I think I know who you are talking about – Eunice and her mother Lois have both joined the Nazarenes here." There was an awkward pause. I gulped, and managed some sort of conventional enquiry as to how they all were; but it seemed as if an invisible curtain had dropped between us, and the spontaneous joy of only a few minutes previously, clouded. It was not undermined, but it suddenly became a precious memory to be treasured, rather than an ongoing pleasure to be enjoyed.

Then ordinariness set in. The relentless grind of everyday life closed down on me like a blanket of fog at sea. I knew that God was still there, just as the sun still shines beyond the swirling banks of mist that part and drift, and thicken and lift, deceiving and confusing; but the vitality and immediacy of the first flush of faith faded and failed, and I felt that I had to drag my faith along with me, instead of being buoyed up and borne along by it, as I had been at first. For six long wearisome years I bumped along the bottom of life. I had no trouble in picking up again the tricks of the tent-making trade; but toiling away at the routine processes of the craft left my mind free to think – and I began to wonder. Why had I been so dramatically confronted by Jesus of Nazareth on the road to Damascus? What was the point of the time I had spent in the desert? Where should I go next – or should I prepare myself for spending the rest of my life in Tarsus? When would I get any kind of indication as to what I should do? Questions gnawed away at me persistently. They generated doubt, and I became aware of its corrosive effects, eating away at the edges of my once so radiant assurance. Of course I meticulously observed the external practice of religion, but often it seemed to be just that – external only, with no inner vitality to it. At the synagogue in Tarsus I came into contact with some intriguing ideas. Merchants whose trade had taken them to Persia came back with the concept that there are two powers in the universe, one good and one evil, and therefore opposed to each other. On the surface this seemed to be an intellectually respectable challenge – it seemed to provide a possible answer to the perennial question as to the origin of evil. Put at its simplest, the indisputable fact of the existence of evil, attested by universal experience, must in the last resort mean one of two things: either God is good, but not omnipotent (for if he were, he would destroy evil); or God is omnipotent, but not good (since he must ultimately have been the origin of evil). But my whole being recoiled instinctively from both of these propositions; for if God is not, among other things, both omnipotent and good, then he cannot be God in any meaningful sense of the term. So I found I had no choice but to reject both these 'solutions', even though that left me with a still unresolved problem. Eventually, however, as I tried to bring my new understanding of God being in Christ to bear on the problem, I began to feel my way towards, not so much a slick, pat answer to a conundrum, as an understanding of how to live with, and benefit from, a creative tension. I wrestled with the idea that God demonstrates his omnipotence by permitting the existence of evil, even though that does not account for the origin of evil; and he demonstrates his goodness by himself entering the arena of human life in the person of Jesus Christ, to combat evil, and to overcome it, even though that does not explain the ongoing agony of human suffering. I found myself rejecting the traditional concept of God sitting in heaven, aloof from the world, and indifferent to the concerns of human life. Instead, I moved toward the idea that in Jesus God had laid aside his Godhead, and had become actively involved in the anguish of human life – not solving all its puzzles by one majestic, irresistible decree from on high, but working from within it, to alleviate its misery by sharing in its suffering, and, most important of all, bearing away its guilt.

Of course these thoughts did not all present themselves to me in one blinding flash of revelation; but reflecting on it all afterwards, I saw that those six years back at home in Tarsus, irksome though they seemed at the time, were a vital preparation for the demanding years that have succeeded them. I was given an opportunity, undistracted by the challenges and responsibilities which have crowded in upon me since then, to hammer out in my own mind the foundations and form of the message I had been given to proclaim. And by the grace of God I was able to take advantage of that opportunity, as I sat cross-legged on the floor in the back of the little workshop I had hired, cutting black cloth woven from goats' hair into the different shapes required for round and tapering tents, or flat and oblong tents, and plying my tent maker's needle to stitch the shapes together, and make holes for poles and cords and guy ropes. I was wholly engrossed in doing just that one fine summer morning, when the sunlight darkened as a shadow fell across my work. I looked up. A large figure loomed black against the brilliant sky. At first glance, looking directly into the light, I could not make out who it was; but then a big bass voice boomed out, "Paul!" Hardly believing my senses, I dropped my work, leapt up, and was promptly engulfed in a hug that lifted me clean off my feet and came close to squeezing the air out of my lungs. With what little breath I had left, I managed to gasp, "Barnabas!"

VI
CHALLENGE

"WHATEVER brings you here?" I squeaked. Barnabas grinned one of his huge grins and kindly let my feet touch the floor again. "The Spirit, speaking through the Church," he replied. Still reeling from the shock of seeing again the man who had been my best, indeed my only, friend when I first became a follower of the Way, I gave up any attempt to follow my usual routine. "I'll shut the shop for the day right away," I said. "Let's go down to the river and find somewhere where we can talk uninterrupted."

To my intense delight I found that Barnabas had not changed one whit. Though we had neither met nor corresponded for more than half a decade, we found we were able to pick up our relationship as if we had parted only yesterday, and carry it forward without a hint of strain or artificiality. But more seemed to have happened to Barnabas than to me during that time. He told me that the believers who had fled from Jerusalem after Stephen was killed had scattered all along the eastern coast of the Great Sea, spreading the Good News about Jesus wherever they went – I felt a hot flush of embarrassment as I recalled that this was exactly what the perceptive trooper had said would happen, when we first chased the Nazarenes out of the Holy City. Initially they had spoken only to fellow Jews; but in the more relaxed atmosphere of Antioch, this new religious movement became the talk of the town, and inquisitive open-minded Greeks began to show interest, and ask questions. To the believers' great surprise, growing numbers of them professed to be convinced, and declared that they too would trust Jesus as Saviour and obey him as Lord. This totally unexpected development had apparently spread like wildfire, and the small, close knit community of believing Jews quickly found themselves swamped by a much larger crowd of Gentiles, all eager to know more, and to be accepted into the fellowship. An urgent plea for advice and help was dispatched to the leaders still in Jerusalem. "That was how I became involved," said Barnabas. "I was delegated to go to Antioch and investigate. I was amazed – and delighted! – at what I found. Hundreds of people were crowding the meetings – sheer numbers had long since forced our people into the market square, so the Gospel was being preached publicly, and winning more adherents every time. The contrast with the furtive, suspicious atmosphere in Jerusalem could not have been greater. Of course, I cannot guarantee that absolutely every single adherent will hold to the faith for the rest of his life; but in no time at all it was obvious to me that this was a genuine movement of the Holy Spirit, and I plunged into the work with grateful enthusiasm. But there are so many people to teach, and such crowds of enquirers all clamouring to know more, that we simply can't cope any more on our own. I was casting around desperately in my mind for a brain-wave, and then I had one – I thought of you! Will you come and help us? The opportunities are literally limitless."

My mind was seething like a maelstrom as he talked. On the face of it this seemed as if it could be the answer to all the bafflement I had felt during the previous six years – perhaps I had been prepared and held in readiness

To be read with
Acts open

D.

for exactly this opportunity. But Gentiles? – non-Jews admitted into the grace of God? I questioned Barnabas closely about this. "Well," he answered, "what other conclusions can we draw? They were responding in hundreds when I left – there could well be thousands of them by the time I get back again. In fact, the need is so urgent, I shall simply have to start my return journey tomorrow – I just can't leave a few brave souls to hold the fort on their own any longer. So what about it – will you come with me?" Silence hung long on the air. I gazed intently at the river flowing slowly and silently past, the merest ripples faintly distorting the image of the leaves reflected from the trees overhead. After receiving no word from the Lord for more than six years, I was being pressed to make a decision in less than six hours – and it was very much more than simply a decision as to whether or not to go to Antioch with Barnabas. It was a decision as to whether or not to repudiate a lifetime's convictions about the uniqueness of God's Chosen People, by associating myself with a trend which, I could have no illusions on the matter, would result certainly in the blurring, and probably the obliteration, of the distinctiveness of the People of the Covenant. Time slid by, as noiseless as the river – and as relentless. A bird chirruped suddenly in the branches above. I turned to look at Barnabas. His face was solemn, his expression respectful, his eyes gravely enquiring – I could see that he was making a conscious effort to exert no pressure on me; but eventually he just quietly asked, "Well?" "I'll come with you," I said, and in less than twelve hours I had made over the business to my father, packed the things I thought I would need for the immediate future, and said farewell to my parents. I never saw either of them again.

We took the coast road from Tarsus to Antioch. It's a good hundred and fifty miles or more, but we had so much to talk about that neither of us noticed the distance. My estimation of Barnabas grew by leaps and bounds as he told me what he had been doing since we parted company so suddenly in Jerusalem, six years previously. The more he told me about what was happening in Antioch, the happier I felt about joining with him in welcoming non-Jews into the fellowship. I had seen Antioch before, when in my late teens I first left Tarsus for Jerusalem; but the impact it made on me when I saw it again was as fresh as if it had been a first sighting. Situated in the wide valley of the river Orontes, about fifteen miles inland from its port of Seleucia, it was set off splendidly by Mount Casius to the south, and the Amanus mountains to the west, while the temple and castle crowning the summit of the mountain finished it off to perfection. I had forgotten how big it was; Barnabas said it was reputed to have a population of half-a-million, and I began to appreciate that its cultural, language and ethnic mix could make it an ideal base from which to spread the Good News about Jesus – provided that it was right to extend the religious privileges of the people of Israel to Romans, Greeks, Chaldaeans, Syrians, and all the other Gentiles teeming in its wide streets, its spacious market places and its shady groves. We were warmly welcomed by the believers there, and were promptly inundated by questions and demands from people of all origins who were intrigued by this new teaching from Judaea, with its insistence that God could be known in a man who had been executed by the Romans, but had returned to life only three days later. It soon became obvious that we were the right people in the right place at the right time; there was a vast spiritual hunger in the Gentile world which was not being met either by the official state religion, or by the mystery cults which seemed to germinate and thrive in the open-minded spirit of enquiry prevailing in Antioch. As a result, the proclamation of Jesus and the resurrection generated immense interest, and we found ourselves talking to never-ending streams of people, from first light to twilight and beyond, every day. It was exhausting but exhilarating. Men and women, young and old, Jews and Gentiles, ranging from the curious through the concerned to the committed, bombarded us with questions and comments and criticisms until we felt totally drained. But there was huge reward for us as well, as increasing numbers of people declared that they were convinced by what we said, and asked to be accepted into the rapidly growing fellowship. We discovered that the talk of the town had thrown up a new name for us; our emphasis on Jesus as God's Chosen One was taken up by the Greek speakers, who used their own word 'Christos' for him, and we soon found ourselves being called Christians. The name stuck immediately, and we have been happy with it ever since.

We were so immersed in taking advantage of the ever expanding opportunities opening up before us, that it came as something of a surprise to be told that there were visitors from Jerusalem asking to see us. One of them in particular made an impression on me. He was a dark, small man, no taller than I, with a brooding intensity about him that seemed to set him apart from the others who came with him. They all announced themselves as prophets in the fellowship of believers in Jerusalem. One Sabbath day soon after they had arrived, the man who had caught my attention stood up in our meeting. Speaking slowly in a low but clear voice, he declared that he was impelled by the Spirit to predict that there would be a severe famine throughout the Roman Empire. His prophecy generated a great deal of interest and discussion, for there were believers in the fellowship who had been told of Jesus' words that famines, among other things, would herald the dawn of a new age when he would return to earth to restore all things to their original perfection, and bring in the long awaited Kingdom of

God. Speculation was intense, and expectation at fever pitch – was Jesus' Second Coming imminent? But I admit to being surprised at the outcome of the debate – the fellowship agreed to make a charity collection for the believers in Jerusalem and Judaea. Despite their declared belief in the early return of Jesus, relatively well-to-do people in Antioch revealed their continuing trust in material things to alleviate the hardships of this life. They were indisputably generous; but the cynical might have suggested that they were prudently providing for the continuation of the life of this world, just in case that of the world to come did not materialise immediately. Be that as it may, Barnabas was entrusted with delivering the proceeds of the collection to the leaders in Jerusalem, and he kindly asked me to accompany him there.

My third visit to the Holy City was very different from the first two. Fourteen years had passed since I was smuggled out in the back of a wagon, and hostility, from the Jews to the Christians in general, and from the Christians to me in particular, had abated. Our journey was uneventful; but the time we spent there was anything but! We heard at first hand a gruesome account of the decapitation, on the orders of King Herod Agrippa, of James, one of the original twelve followers of Jesus; and we marvelled at the miraculous way in which Peter had been freed from gaol on the very night before he was due to go on trial, with the death sentence a foregone conclusion. The details were vividly related to us by Mark, who was fully informed about the whole affair because it was to his mother's house that Peter first came immediately after his escape – and it was Mark's mother who put us up while we were in Jerusalem. It is likely that our visit did not draw the attention it might just otherwise have done, because it was overshadowed by the state visit of Queen Helena of Adiabene to King Herod Agrippa. The usual stir of excitement generated by such events was heightened on this occasion when Queen Helena, in a well publicised act of political generosity, arranged for corn to be imported from Egypt, and distributed to the hungry inhabitants of the Holy City – we were pleased that the believers there were helped by fellow followers of the Way, three hundred and fifty miles or more to the north. But the most significant development in our short stay in Jerusalem was the growing interest in our work shown by Mark. He was an attractive young man, with a superb physique, and an enviably relaxed, laid back attitude to life. At the same time he exuded an infectious enthusiasm for whatever caught his interest. A ready smile revealed marvellously white even teeth; and no one seemed able to resist the sparkling eyes with which he engaged and held their gaze. Even I, aloof though I am reputed to be, could not help but warm to the appealing eagerness of youth which he embodied. Despite all this, however, or perhaps even because of it, I could not shake off a tiny indefinable sense of unease about him; but this was comprehensively submerged when he launched a high powered bid to be allowed to come back with us to Antioch. As he was also Barnabas' cousin, I felt entirely comfortable with the idea – though unspoken, it was assumed that his older relative would take responsibility for him; and Barnabas commented privately to me that it would be no bad thing for Mark to move out of his mother's home, and start to establish an identity and a life of his own. So where two of us had left Antioch, three of us returned there, not much more than a month later.

Antioch is more than twice the distance of Damascus from Jerusalem; but between the three of us there was so much to talk about that we were hardly aware of either the distance, or the time it took us to cover it. I rapidly discovered that I had much to learn from Mark. He chatted non-stop, seemingly about whatever came into his handsome head; but it was not difficult to guide him into talking about what I wanted to know. I had already realised that Mark had been in a unique position to learn about Jesus – his mother's comfortable house in Jerusalem, large enough to accommodate gatherings of scores of people at a time, had become the de facto headquarters of the Nazarene movement in the city, and the bright and inquisitive teenager had had unparalleled opportunities to talk with and listen to people who had met the Lord, heard him teach, watched him heal, seen him die, and met him again after death. Mark was moreover a close friend and confidant of Peter, and he related his memories of what Peter had told him about people and places and events, with a vividness and an eye for detail that was patently genuine; not even the most creative imagination could have generated the multi-dimensional pictures he was able to convey to us in words. As a result, my own understanding of Jesus developed significantly; I saw him now as the mighty Saviour, but also as the humble, suffering servant Whose death on the cross effected an irreversible reconciliation between sinful humanity and Holy God. Back again at Antioch, we found the Way as vigorous as ever, surging ahead, and the number of Followers growing by leaps and bounds. So incessant were the demands made by new converts upon the leaders of the movement, that we found it essential to withdraw from the hurly-burly of the meeting place at a set time each day, to renew our own spiritual strength in prayer and fellowship, and ministry to each other. Those were precious oases of calm in the stress and clamour of trying to channel and utilise the raw enthusiasm of young believers, all eager to savour to the full the new reality they were experiencing. One searingly hot summer day five of us had withdrawn to a small room at the back of the house which had become the focus of our work in Antioch. It was toward the middle of the day. The morning had been as hectic as any; but the oppressive heat had sapped the energies of the crowds thronging the street outside and ruthlessly pushing into the already packed courtyard, and a lull settled over the house. Some sat on the ground in the shade of the south flank of the building; but most had drifted out through the big wooden doors that gave directly onto the street, and for a blessed hour or so, peace descended. In the stifling heat of the small room Niger, Lucius, Manaen, Barnabas and I, seated cross-legged on mats on the floor, started as usual by sharing questions and answers, problems and prayers; but our conversation became more desultory, until at length we lapsed into silence. But it was not the silence of exhaustion and sleep – on the contrary, it was very much the opposite. We became aware of an energy gathering in the room, of a power sparking between us, of an exalted state of consciousness which lifted us up, out of ourselves, onto a level of receptiveness of God such as we agreed afterwards we had never known before. There came a low moaning sound, which steadily rose in intensity until a blast of wind slammed into the house with a ferocity which, had it been merely natural, would certainly have flattened the building. The walls creaked and shook, the roof timbers strained to be freed from their ties – and then the ground moved. The shriek of the wind was lost in the rolling thunder of an earthquake which rumbled and roared and ricocheted from side to side of the room in rhythmic surges – and yet nothing was damaged or broken. Fire flared and flames flashed from one to another of us – yet nothing was burned. We all fell flat on our faces on the floor, instinctively at first, as though to avoid physical injury, but then as a deliberate act of prostration, for we all knew that we had been visited by the Spirit, the Holy Spirit of Very God himself, and in his presence we could only abhor ourselves, and repent in dust and ashes. For as the wind died away, the dust it had disturbed slowly settled down again, and the ashes of the fire which had burnt nothing were there on the floor, still hot to the touch; and even as we lay prone we detected one last, small jolt, deep in the ground beneath us. Afterwards there was a stillness so profound, and a silence so deep, as none of us was willing to violate, until, in the cool of the evening, the familiar voice of young Mark broke in on our rapture. "Barnabas! Paul! What are you doing here?"

It was a bright and breezy morning as Barnabas, Mark and I stood on the quayside at Seleucia. Two days before we had been charged by the church in Antioch with responsibility for taking the Good News about Jesus overseas for the very first time. We had no qualms about this at all – we knew without a shadow of doubt that this was what the Spirit of God intended for us; and the leaders of the Fellowship had underscored our conviction by laying their hands on us and praying for us, in a simple but solemn commissioning ceremony. There was no problem over our destination, either – Barnabas was as excited as a school boy at the thought of returning to his beloved native Cyprus. So we struck a deal with the captain of a merchantman bound for Salamis, on the east coast of the island; and eventually, after the inevitable delays over the stowing and restowing of cargo, and the haggling over harbour dues and passengers' fares, we weighed anchor, and took a southwest bearing for our destination. I grinned to myself at the green apprehension on Mark's face as we left the shelter of the land astern, and the ship began to respond to the slap of the wind and the swell of the waves; but he seemed to find his sea legs pretty quickly, and was soon his joyously irrepressible self again. It was not long before we had crossed the hundred miles or so of open sea between Syria and Cyprus, and reached the relative shelter of the long northeast finger of the island. The nights were decidedly chilly, but the days were sunny and warm; and in the brisk, bracing breeze we all felt rested and restored after the draining demands of the work at Antioch. Draining it certainly had been; but as we talked it over together at our leisure, we all agreed that we had learnt tremendously from the experience, and by the time we tied up at the quayside at Salamis, we were eager to shape our approach to the people there in line with the lessons we thought we had been taught. Rarely have I been so rapidly disillusioned.

It goes without saying that habit is a very valuable aid to everyday life. It can free the mind from the drudgery of consciously thinking through each one of the multitude of mundane matters that crop up in the regular routines of existence; but like so many other aids to help us along our way, what is an excellent servant can all too easily become a tyrannical master. Thus – or so it seemed to me – it was an altogether helpful habit that prompted us to ask the way to the local synagogue on our very first Sabbath day in Salamis; but I was wholly unprepared for the unrelenting hold of habit over the minds and attitudes of the people in the synagogue. Here were devout Jews, unswerving in their lifelong loyalty to the faith of the Fathers, patiently waiting for the fulfilment of the promise repeatedly made from the times of the Patriarchs onwards, that God would send his people a Deliverer, stolidly unmoved when we proclaimed to them that God had kept his word, and that the Messiah had come. I and my companions were staggered at the lack, not only of response to, but even of interest in, what we said. It had been the habit of a lifetime, the ingrained habit of successive generations, to hear the promise of God read from the Scriptures, week in, week out, year on year, decade after decade – now it seemed that endless repetition had numbed their sensitivity, deadened their receptiveness, atrophied their ability to respond. I gazed in uncomprehending disbelief at the sea of expressionless faces in front of me. There was no hostility, no antagonism, no amused mockery – just dull, blank indifference. It was as though they were seeing me only dimly, as if through a heavy veil. Afterwards, a few of the older members of the synagogue made conventional courteous comments to us – asking after our health, talking about the weather, and so forth; but not one single solitary person made any reference to the love of God, or the grace of Jesus Christ, or the fellowship of the Holy Spirit, which Barnabas and I had set forth with all the passion at our command.

The whole atmosphere of our venture changed. Bewilderment replaced the eager anticipation with which we had set out. We had proclaimed exactly the same message – why was there such a total difference in response between enthusiastic inquisitiveness in Antioch, and lethargic apathy in Salamis? In fact, the answer to our question was as obvious as the sun at noon-day; but we each sensed that the other was unwilling to be the first to broach it, and it was Mark who finally brought out into the open what we were both wrestling with privately. "Of course," he said, airily unaware of the vast implications of what he was saying, "the people who responded so encouragingly in Antioch were mostly Gentile God-fearers, weren't they? The people we have spoken to here have all been Jews, haven't they?" Relieved that what we had been reluctant to face up to had been so innocently set right in front of us, we fell to discussing our strategy for the future. Almost inevitably, perhaps, we split three ways. I could not erase from my mind what Ananias had told me of Jesus' words to him when he visited me in Straight Street in Damascus; he had initially protested at being asked to minister to me, but he later confided that the Lord had said to him, "Go! This man is my chosen instrument to carry my name before the Gentiles." Mark, on the other hand, proved to be unexpectedly conservative – but I immediately understood why. He had been brought up in the capital city of Judaism, and all his formative experiences of the Way had been in the context of the Jerusalem believers – it was hardly surprising that he counselled taking the Good News of the Messiah to the Jews whose whole culture was coloured by the expectation of his coming. His arguments were frequently backed up by references to what Peter thought, what Peter said, what Peter did. Poor Barnabas was torn between the two of us – he sympathised with Mark because he too had been for several years at the heart of the Jewish fellowship in Jerusalem; but he could not deny the reality of what he had experienced at Antioch, when he had been overjoyed at the sight of Gentiles turning to faith in Jesus, in such numbers that he had had to fetch me from Tarsus to help with the flood of new converts. So debate swung back and forth between us, until we agreed to try again in another town.

People in power seem to attract assorted hangers-on and would-be parasites as irresistibly as a lamp attracts moths. We ran into a cluster of such people buzzing around the Roman administrative headquarters in Paphos, all of them anxious to catch the eye and the favour of the Roman proconsul. One of them latched onto us as soon as we took a stand in the market place and started to talk about Jesus. An involuntary shiver went down my spine when I first felt his gaze fix on me; and when I turned to look at him, I was locked into a steely stare which promptly became a hostile challenge. An instantaneous, wholly irrational, antagonism seemed to spark between us. I turned away – and immediately sensed the humiliation of defeat; when I stole another look in his direction, his lips curled into a mocking sneer, and there was a gleam of triumph in his unsmiling eyes. I felt surprisingly unsettled. But when I asked about him afterwards, my surprise lessened. It transpired that he claimed to be a kind of sorcerer, and his stabs at foretelling the future had apparently been shrewd enough to make some sort of impression on Sergius Paulus, the Proconsul. The sorcerer's hostility to us was instinctive – and well grounded. He obviously knew that his place in the Proconsul's favour was founded on fraud, and he feared exposure to the light of truth. Only three days after our arrival in Paphos we were sitting under the shade of the orange trees in the market square, when a young Roman officer approached. With ostentatious military swagger, he halted in front of us, and saluted. "His Excellency the Proconsul greets you," he said. "He has heard that you are proclaiming a new way of life. I am commanded to inform you that he would like to know more about it. He therefore invites you to accompany me to his residence." Subdued comment rippled momentarily across the crowd surrounding us. We got to our feet. "We are honoured by his Excellency's kind invitation," I said, as calmly as I could, though inwardly I felt a rush of excitement at this completely unexpected opportunity apparently opening up before us. "We shall be delighted to accept it." The correct young man again saluted, and turned on his heel. Barnabas, Mark and I followed him to the imposing Roman administrative complex dominating the town from its hillside position. We mounted the wide sweep of steps to a shallow portico, where sentries on duty at either side of the door into the building presented arms as our escort passed them. Our sandals seemed to flap embarrassingly loudly as we crossed the atrium, where the white flagstone floor gave off a welcome coolness; and then we were in a small side room where the Proconsul was seated at a table, frowning at some papers in his hand. There was one other person there – the sorcerer who had silently challenged us in the market square was sitting at the side of the table. The Proconsul rose to meet us and proffered his hand in greeting; out of the corner of my eye I saw Elymas, the sorcerer, also reluctantly stand. The young subaltern took his stand behind the Proconsul's chair, where he maintained unflinching watch throughout our entire meeting.

Sergius Paulus motioned us to seat ourselves, and got the encounter off to an easy start with his comment that he and I shared the same surname. I seized the opportunity to say that there was more – much, much more – that I would like to share with him, if he were willing. We talked all through the afternoon. It was immediately obvious, from his comments and questions, that the Proconsul of the Province of Cyprus was no run-of-the-mill military man. "This is a peaceful island," he explained, "and my duties are far from onerous. I have a golden opportunity to ponder life's deepest questions, and," with a wry glance at Elymas, "to investigate some proposed responses to those questions." Elymas smirked unconvincingly. Barnabas nodded to me, so I took up the reins. I spoke of the one God, the only God, Maker of all that is. I spoke of human beings, made by him in his own likeness, with freedom of choice; but marring that likeness, and breaking their communion with him and with each other by making wrong choices. Sergius Paulus listened intently, interjecting occasionally with impressive intelligence and surprising knowledge. I rapidly warmed to a man with whom I could so easily relate; but my growing rapport with him was matched by a palpably rising anger in Elymas, until, when I spoke of Jesus as God's gracious answer to humanity's deepest needs, the sorcerer could contain himself no longer. "This is all arrant nonsense, Your Excellency," he burst out. "Whoever heard such patent rubbish? You should banish this man and his colleagues from your Province forthwith." I waited for the Proconsul to respond. After several moments of silence, Sergius Paulus slowly turned in his chair and looked long and hard at Elymas. "What I have heard this afternoon," he said, "has touched depths in me that all your magic and mumbo-jumbo have never come anywhere near arousing. What answer have you to my guilty conscience? What reassurance can you offer me about death, and the afterlife?" Acutely aware that he was now on the defensive, the sorcerer changed his approach; but that very tactic signalled that he knew his position was weak, and it was rapidly all too obvious that he had no answers to the Proconsul's questions – indeed, he seemed to be unable to comprehend the level on which the latter's mind was working. His attempted response faltered and floundered;

so with no great subtlety he turned to attack us and our message. I listened in silence to his bombast and bluster. The pool of bright sunlight through the circular window moved slowly but surely across the floor; and then, as the sun began to dip towards the west, the circle of light rose from the floor, bathing the Proconsul's table in liquid gold until the moment came when it reached Elymas' face. He suddenly found himself staring directly into the brilliance of the unclouded sun. The flow of his diatribe was briefly interrupted, and I seized the moment. "You are a child of the devil, and an enemy of everything that is right!" I thundered. "You are full of all kinds of deceit and trickery. Will you never stop perverting the right ways of the Lord? Now the hand of the Lord is against you. You are going to be blind, and for a time you will be unable to see the light of the sun." The sorcerer emitted a low moan, and lurched against the table. With his left hand over his eyes, he flailed about with his right hand, wildly seeking for something to hold on to. The Proconsul's aide-de-camp stepped forward, took him by the elbow, and led him out of the room. Sergius Paulus eyed the three of us with a mixture of amazement and awe. "Tell me more," he whispered. He clapped his hands once, and the ADC brought in a huge basket of fresh fruit, silver goblets, pitchers of wine, and oil lamps for the table. The lamps burned long into the night as the three of us took the Pronconsul deeper into the facts of the faith, and its implications for every individual adherent. I noticed with amusement that it was the younger men – Mark, and the Proconsul's subaltern – who first succumbed to yawns of weariness. We were called back to the Residency several times in the ensuing days; and when we finally set sail from Paphos for Perga in Pamphylia, it was in the exhilarating knowledge that a man of intelligence and intellectual stature, as well as professional and social standing, had made a declaration of faith in Jesus as Lord.

VII
RESPONSE

"PAUL! Paul! Wake up, Paul! Have you seen this?" I became vaguely aware that my right shoulder was being roughly shaken. I half opened one eye, and promptly shut it again. "Go away, Barnabas," I mumbled, "I'm not awake yet." "Well, you jolly well should be," my very good friend hissed in my right ear. "The sun's been up for ages already – and look what I've found." I made a half-hearted effort to pull the blanket right over my head; but Barnabas would have none of it. "Read this," he ordered, fairly pushing a scrap of papyrus into my face. I sighed wearily, but could make nothing of the blur of handwriting on the papyrus. "Barnabas," I remonstrated, "you know my sight is poor at the best of times – and seconds after being rudely awoken from sleep is very far from being the best of times. What does it say?" Barnabas' face assumed a portentous expression. "Mark has gone", he solemnly declared. "Gone? What do you mean, 'gone'? Gone where?" I asked. "Mark has gone back home. I found this message on his mat when I got up myself, not five minutes ago. He says he has decided to return to Jerusalem – no reason given, no apology offered – nothing; no sign of any of his belongings, either. He must have waited until we were both asleep last night, and then taken himself off. Goodness knows how he'll get there – he's got virtually no money. I suppose he'll either work his passage on a ship, or rely on getting lifts from friendly travellers on the roads. But I'm worried about him – what lies behind this, I wonder?"

By now, of course, I was wide awake and sitting bolt upright. I could understand Barnabas' concern for his young cousin – but I was not at all sure that I could understand Mark. I felt badly let down, as much by the manner of his going as by the fact of it; and I said so, in no uncertain terms. Barnabas loyally did his best to soften the blow by seeking to account for it. He wondered whether Mark had been disillusioned by our total failure to make any impact in Salamis, or perhaps disconcerted by the sinister opposition of Elymas in Paphos – to which I retorted that he must surely have realised that a message for which Stephen had been stoned and James beheaded, would certainly arouse comparable hostility; but even so, the conversion of Sergius Paulus should have been of sufficient encouragement to him to go on with the mission. At the very least he should have talked over with either or both of us whatever it was that was bothering him, instead of just leaving us in the lurch like that. Barnabas shrugged his shoulders and said no more; so I had perforce to let the matter drop.

In sombre mood, we agreed that we would not stay in Perga, but try to restart our endeavour in the other Antioch, the main town in Pisidia, fifty miles or more to the north. We trudged wearily up the steep track-ways which zig-zagged to and fro to climb the scarp-face of the Taurus mountains; but it was a relief to leave behind the enervating climate of the low-lying coastland. When we finally breasted the crest we were rewarded with a vast panorama of undulating country stretching away in front of us for as far as we could see, broken by lines of hills and valleys, with wooded glens providing variety and interest. It was the eve of the Sabbath when we eventually reached our destination, so we were perfectly content to sit quietly in the synagogue next day; but we were not allowed to pass unnoticed. After the readings from the Law and the Prophets, the president fixed his eye on us and said, "Brothers, if you have a message of encouragement for the people, please speak." That was exactly what we needed. An invitation to give encouragement provided us with just the encouragement we ourselves needed. Barnabas nodded at me, and without more ado I stood up and launched eagerly into an account of what God had done for his Chosen People, culminating in the gift of his Child Jesus, through Whom the forgiveness of sins is proclaimed. The upshot was intriguing; the meeting ended with an invitation to speak again on the following Sabbath day, and the intervening week was filled with visits from interested people, Jews and Gentiles, wanting to know more. The response was not as enthusiastic as it had been in Antioch in Syria, but it could not have been further from the apathy we had met with in Salamis in Cyprus.

Accordingly, seven days later we set out from our lodgings, in good time to be at the synagogue for the start of the service. There were surprising numbers of people thronging the street; and we were greeted with gratifying respect as soon as we appeared. The crowd then moved after us as we began to make our way toward the synagogue, and it slowly dawned on us that they were heading for the same destination. When we got there, the president asked us if we would mind speaking out-of-doors, as there was no hope of accommodating in the building all the people who wanted to hear us. My heart missed a beat with excitement at the thought that almost the entire population of the place was eager to hear more of the truth of God; but my elation was short lived. The same old congenital fault line in the human race showed up almost straightaway – not the biological difference between men and women, nor the economic distinction between freemen and slaves, but the even more significant racial division between Jews and Gentiles. In no time at all we found ourselves up against hostility from the champions of the Chosen People. It cut me to the quick, not to be contradicted, and that in public, but to be opposed by the very people for whom the Good News of Jesus was intended. An impromptu public debate developed, and the customary hour of worship was rapidly outstripped as argument and counter argument swayed back and forth between us and our adversarial fellow Jews. As the afternoon wore on the tone of the debate degenerated into antagonism and abuse. Barnabas and I asked for a respite. We used the brief break for an urgent discussion as to the line we should take in view of the unexpected turn the event had taken. In retrospect we saw it as one of the decisive moments in our whole ministry, when we agreed to say that we were duty bound to proclaim first to the People of the Covenant what God had done; but since they seemed determined to reject our message, thereby pronouncing themselves to be unworthy of the eternal life which that message offered them, we would turn to the Gentiles. We declared that we were implementing a prophecy made by Isaiah, when he said of the coming Chosen One, 'I have made you a light for the Gentiles, that you may bring salvation to the ends of the earth.' Understandably, our Gentile hearers were hugely encouraged by this, and they soon outnumbered the Jews in the company of people who professed themselves to be persuaded by what they had heard, and asked to be baptised, to signify their adherence to the Way.

But almost inevitably, our success in Antioch in Pisidia generated its own backlash. Hard-line orthodox Jews set about manipulating the levers of influence in the social structure of the city, and we soon found ourselves up against the entrenched power-bloc which exercised an all-pervasive control, more deep seated and more far reaching, even than that of the occupying Roman authorities. Women at the centre of intricate networks of relationships were coaxed or cajoled into disapproving of us; and they demonstrated the effectiveness of their position in the community by goading the city fathers into declaring us to be *persona non grata*.

A pattern began to emerge. Thrown out of Antioch, we headed for Iconium, sixty or so miles away, a city of luxuriant gardens in an otherwise high waterless plain. Here, too, we enjoyed initial success, speaking first in the local synagogue, and meeting with a gratifying wave of enthusiastic response; but then, as at Antioch, dyed-in-the-wool traditionalists in the local Jewish community engineered a reaction against us. But there were variations within the overall pattern. At Iconium we were granted the grace of signs and miracles. We were greatly encouraged by this open endorsement of the message we were proclaiming; but we were equally taken aback by the fact that by no means was everybody convinced by them. So we decided to dig our heels in, and make more of a stand at Iconium than we had done at Antioch. We stayed there for some considerable time, teaching the believers all we knew of the Way, and continuing to attract new converts as well; but eventually antagonism became explicit. Sharp-eared sympathisers picked up details of a plan to intimidate us by means of physical violence, even, perhaps, stoning. So, reckoning that we would be more useful alive than dead, we left Iconium, and walked to Lystra.

Perhaps it was the fact that we were able to walk there which concentrated my mind on a lame man whom we saw sitting under a tree in the town square. Barnabas started talking to a knot of men gathered there on the day after we arrived. The lame man was listless and dejected, hardly bothering to solicit alms from the passers-by – they must have seen him every day of their lives, and he presumably knew from long experience who would respond to his need, and who would not. I watched with growing fascination the effect of Barnabas' preaching on this man. First he lifted his head; then, painfully slowly, he shifted his position so that he could look directly at Barnabas. When I took over from Barnabas I felt my attention irresistibly drawn to this one individual. Though there was a sizeable crowd listening, they seemed to be blocked out of my mind – and I could see that my uncontrived concentration on the lame man was fully reciprocated by him. A tension was being generated between us which could not simply be ignored – ultimately, something must happen; so, ultimately, I gazed directly into his eyes and, prompted by the Spirit, I said, "Stand up straight on your feet." There was not a moment's hesitation. With an agility a teenager would envy, the lame man leapt lightly to his feet, and moved lithely through the crowd to kneel in front of us. We pulled him sharply to his feet, and began to explain that it was by faith in the Name of Jesus that he had been healed; but someone shouted, "The gods have come down to us in human form!" and we could scarcely make ourselves heard above the hullabaloo that instantly broke out from the crowd. People at the front were prostrating themselves on the ground, while a section of the crowd broke away and raced towards the city gates. We struggled in vain to instil some sort of sanity into the souls in front of us, but they were not to be calmed; and then, in what seemed like no time at all, there was an impromptu religious procession bearing down upon us. Lowing oxen, their eyes dilated in terror, and with garlands of flowers and evergreen leaves round their necks or stuck rakishly on their horns, were being pushed and pulled along the street, with a priest leaping excitedly about in front of them. I caught a flash of sunlight glinting off a murderously long blade – and there was no longer any possibility of doubting the priest's intentions, and those of the mob with him. In the deafening hubbub filling the market square there were unmistakable shouts of "Jupiter!" and "Mercury!" and we realised with spine-chilling horror that we were not to be sacrificed, but sacrificed to, as gods. We plunged headlong into the heart of the surging mass of people, both of us spontaneously ripping our cloaks as we went. Taken aback by this unexpected display of human weakness, the crowd began to sober down, until we were eventually able to make ourselves heard. "What is this that you are doing?" I bawled. "We are only human beings," roared Barnabas, "no less mortal than you. The Good News we bring tells you to turn from these follies to the Living God." The expression on the little priest's face visibly darkened; and I experienced an ominous premonition of trouble brewing when I saw a group of Jews sidle up and engage him in conversation. With a start of alarm I recognised some of them – they had been ringleaders of the opposition to us in Antioch and Iconium. I affected not to be rattled by them; but try as I might, I could not resist stealing anxious glances at them – and it was abundantly clear that they were deliberately attempting to intimidate us by staring at us with open hostility. With a sickening, sinking feeling, I sensed that the advantage lay with them. It was soon apparent that they had won over the local priest, and persuaded him to use his influence with the townspeople to turn them against us. The believers, too, realised that the mood of the crowd was changing – and changing fast; they begged us to move away from a rapidly developing confrontation, but Barnabas and I were both reluctant to be cowed by devotees of paganism. Seeing the indecision in our little group, the crowd facing us broke ranks and rushed towards us. Instinctively but ingloriously, we turned tail and fled. Then the worst possible thing happened – unable to keep up with the others, I got cut off, and found myself trapped by an exultantly crowing gang of ruffians.

Even so, the first stone came as a fearful shock. It struck me from behind, fair and square between the shoulder blades. With no chance of seeing it coming, I succumbed helplessly to its force, and fell flat on my face. With a yell of triumph the gang closed in, and for what seemed like an eternity stones large and small rained down upon me – arms, legs, back, no part of me was spared except for my head, which I was able to cover with my arms. But I was bruised and cut and bleeding, and had no strength to resist when I was savagely hauled along the ground, through the town gate and, in a final gesture of contempt, unceremoniously flung onto the public rubbish dump outside. Ostentatiously dusting off their hands, my tormentors returned noisily to the town; but despite my pain and humiliation, I had the most vivid recollection of Stephen's expression and voice as he collapsed under a hail of stones for daring to be a follower of Jesus. With my face pushed right into the most nauseating mess of putrefaction, I rallied myself with the thought that all is far outweighed by the gain of knowing Christ Jesus my Lord, for whose sake I lose everything – I count it so much garbage for the sake of gaining Christ and finding myself incorporate in him. All I care for is to know Christ, to experience the power of his resurrection, and to share in his suffering, in growing conformity with his death, if only I may finally arrive at the resurrection from the dead. And then I experienced a resurrection of sorts, as some of the younger men among the believers came running up and gently helped me to my feet and supported me on each side as I stumbled slowly and painfully into a welcoming family's home for the night. Solicitous with warm water and clean cloths, soothing oil and fortifying wine, they ensured that I had healing sleep. Barnabas was there too, clucking as anxiously over me as a hen over her chicks. "Do you feel fit enough to travel?" he asked. "It would be unfair of us to draw hostile attention to these good people by staying here any longer, you know." I still disliked giving the impression of running away, but I accepted the wisdom of his advice; so with a heavy heart, as well as many involuntary groans of pain from me, we left Lystra and sought sanctuary in Derbe, about thirty miles to the south-east. The people there proved to be as ready for the Good News as any we had met on the whole of our journey thus far, and it came as a real shot in the arm to observe them listening attentively, and responding eagerly, to the message of peace with God through faith in Jesus. I despised myself for wondering apprehensively whether the opponents who had pursued us so relentlessly from town to town would arrive in Derbe too; but they did not appear, and we were able to establish an enthusiastic fellowship of believers there. Their joy in their newfound faith was infectious, and Barnabas and I both felt our courage returning as we saw again the power of the Spirit making new men and women, changed out of all recognition from the cowardly, cynical, conscienceless people they had previously been. Numerous patently genuine conversions revived our confidence in the Gospel as the saving power of God for every one who has faith – the Jew first, but the Gentile also – because here is revealed God's way of righting wrong, a way that starts from faith and ends in faith; as Scripture says, 'He shall gain life who is justified through faith.'

So it came as no surprise at all to either of us when at breakfast one morning we both simultaneously broached the idea of going back to the towns we had already visited, despite the very varied receptions we had met with. It was immensely heartening to each of us to find our personal wonderings validated by the other's. We agreed that we must make it abundantly clear that we were not daunted by opposition; but more importantly, we felt the need to encourage the newly established churches in each of the places we had visited. So we retraced our steps; but we used a different tactic this time. Instead of heading straight for places of public assembly, such as town squares or market places, as we had done on our outward journey, we went to the homes of people in Lystra, Iconium and Antioch who had professed trust in Jesus when we first preached there. Although they were only a matter of months into their new life, virtually all of them seemed as keen as they were when they were first converted; so Barnabas and I took a deep breath and appointed Elders in each little group. We reasoned that mature people would not only be a help in nurturing the newborn faith of others, but would themselves be developed by the responsibility of overseeing them, and caring for them. It was exhilarating to think that there were now lively little Christian churches in four of the towns of southern Galatia; and I confessed to Barnabas that I had been guilty of trepidation when we returned to the places where we had met with opposition and maltreatment. "Well," he responded, with his characteristic forthrightness, "the best cure for that is to go straight into the situation that you think is threatening, and face up to it, knowing that God is with you. We'll retrace our steps to Perga, and this time we'll proclaim the Good News there." I knew Barnabas well enough by now to appreciate that this was no outburst of blustering self confidence. He was a man who walked more closely with God than anyone else I had met, so I was totally content to go along with his proposal. We made the long journey south through the mountains of Pisidia and Pamphylia, and took our stand in the centre of Perga to preach Jesus

Christ and him crucified. We were heard with respectful interest, and there was not the slightest indication of even a hint of opposition. I thanked God for the faith of my fellow follower of the Way; he was indeed a 'Son of Exhortation'.

When we sensed that we had done as much as we usefully could in Perga, we travelled down to the coast at Attalia, and soon found a ship bound for Seleucia. A steady westerly meant that we made good progress; but the sky was clouded all the way, and wisps of storm-wrack scudded ominously below the grey cloud base. This time it was Barnabas' turn to be apprehensive – he was noticeably quiet throughout the whole of the voyage. The sea was running in long crests and deep troughs, which gave the ship a most unsettling motion – Barnabas would probably have felt better if he could have been sick; but he wasn't, and no one on board was more grateful than he when we finally made the shelter of the harbour at Seleucia. I experienced a tingling sense of excitement at seeing again the familiar hills and valleys surrounding Antioch; and the comforting glow of reassurance was reinforced by the warmth of the brothers' and sisters' greetings when we met again with the church which had sent us out on our mission nearly two years earlier. Inevitably there were excited exchanges of news on both sides; but what emerged as of most significance was the fact that we had met with continuing response to the Gospel by Gentiles. It seemed that we had been guided to return to Antioch at a crucial moment – we had only been back a matter of days when some Jewish believers arrived from Judaea. They promptly put paid to the euphoria of our homecoming – they were very insistent that salvation depended not only on acknowledging that Jesus is the Messiah, but also on full observance of all the rites of the Jewish faith – including circumcision for all male believers. They maintained that

Jesus is the crown and consummation of Judaism, not its replacement; he himself was a Jew, and had been circumcised, and therefore all his followers should not merely have to, but would actually want to, follow his example in this respect, if they claimed to be genuine believers. It was a powerful argument; but the Gentile converts at Antioch objected that it made acceptance into the new Church of the Christians conditional on conformity with a religion which, though it was certainly attractive to many, was alien to more.

It was at this point that Barnabas and I entered into the controversy. We had listened carefully to what the brothers from Judaea had to say; but the whole weight of our experience over the preceding two years militated against distorting the free act of faith by forcing it into the narrow restriction of ritual observance. Debate was long and hard. Days often overflowed into nights as discussion swayed back and forth; and sometimes, under the pressure of profoundly-felt convictions, it degenerated into heated argument, and fierce dissension. Eventually the only agreement to emerge between the two points of view was that here was a matter of principle too important to be settled by just one provincial outcrop of the church – it must be referred to the leaders of the whole Christian community, in Jerusalem. Barnabas and I were obvious choices to represent the Gentile believers, and two of the brothers from Judaea – like me, Pharisees – were charged to put the opposing view. We travelled together amicably enough, though I was intrigued to observe the spontaneous delight of Christians in the little congregations in Phoenicia and Samaria when we told them of Gentiles accepting the faith in the course of our recent journey.

Jerusalem was as stimulating as ever. It was a stirring experience to meet again with people who had actually lived and talked and worked with Jesus, had watched him endure inconceivable agony as he sank, painfully slowly, into bitter death, cruelly suspended, naked, on nails to the mocking gaze of heartless passers-by – and then, in unimaginable ecstasy, had met him again when he came back to them after death. There was an air of solemnity about the assembly in which the issue at stake was considered. The meeting was held in the large upper room of Mark's mother's house, already familiar to me from my previous visit. More than a hundred people had gathered there by the time we arrived; and when Peter and James appeared, all conversation ceased, and everyone stood up. We sang a Psalm, and prayer was offered. Then followed a long debate; but I was relieved that it remained on a high level of dignity and courtesy throughout, even though the proponents of the opposing points of view expounded their positions with fervour and passion. The dazzling sunlight made a fascinating diamond-shaped pattern on the floor as it streamed through the trellis-work outside the open windows, and then imperceptibly drifted onto tunics and head-dresses as it slowly began to lessen in intensity. The discussion was gripping – there was not the slightest chance of losing interest as speaker after speaker rose, with varying volume of voice, differing dialects, strange stresses, and arresting rhythms, holding us all spellbound. Hardly anyone noticed when, as the golden light of evening gradually faded, young Mark slipped quietly through the door and with swift and silent grace moved from lamp to lamp, lighting each one from the flaming torch in his hand. Eventually there emerged the sense that the whole question had been fully aired and comprehensively discussed. Calm and silence descended. The deepening quiet seemed all of a piece with the darkening night. The sounds of the city outside subsided, and in the solemn silence every soul sensed that the Spirit was present. In wonder we worshipped and waited. Even breathing seemed an unwarrantable intrusion into the exquisite ecstasy of the experience of the presence of God. There was no noise, no movement, no external manifestation to seize upon; but there was utter stillness, timeless tranquillity, supreme serenity. This was not the suspension of human responsibility, the overriding of human integrity, the negation, even temporarily, of human personality; rather, it was the entire taking-up of every human capability, the utilisation to its fullest extent of every human capacity, the total satisfaction of every human competence in the highest and alone-fulfilling activity humans can undertake – the contemplation of Very God himself, Who in eternal felicity alone holds sway, King of kings and Lord of lords, alone possessing immortality, alone dwelling in unapproachable light, Whom no one has ever seen, or ever can see.

In the end, words – few at first, and so quietly spoken as to be barely audible – broke through to illuminate the mystery of our communion with the Most Holy, just as stars break through the darkness of the night to guide the seeking traveller. In a slow, grave voice Peter told the assembly of his experience of the grace of God in the conversion of Cornelius, a centurion in the Italian Cohort; and of how the Treasurer of the Queen of Ethiopia had responded to Philip's preaching of the Gospel. Then Barnabas and I related the signs and miracles God had worked through us among the Gentiles. Finally, James spoke. He picked up Peter's theme that God had shown his approval of the Gentiles by giving the Holy Spirit to them as much as he had done to us – he had made no difference between them and us, for he had purified their hearts by faith, as well as ours. James concluded that there was therefore no ground for imposing irksome restrictions on Gentiles who were turning to God through faith in Jesus; but with profound wisdom and sensitivity he proposed that a letter of encouragement be sent to all the churches with Gentile members, with advice on how to conduct themselves in the pagan environments in which they lived. The meeting asked Barsabbas and Silas, two prominent men in the church in Jerusalem, to accompany Barnabas and me back to Antioch, to endorse the validity of the copy of the letter which we took with us. We travelled north by the coastal road, and once again met with a heartwarming reception from the Christians in Antioch. Barsabbas and Silas were an inspired choice. Just when the church at Antioch was getting used to Barnabas and me, and even developing a mild immunity to our teaching, two fresh faces from Jerusalem injected a new vitality into the believers' lives, which made the church in the northern city at least as powerful a witness for Christ as was the church in the south. With the question hanging over the acceptance of the Gentiles now resolved, there was another surge in the growth of the church; and when Barsabbas eventually returned to Jerusalem, he was able to take yet more encouraging news with him. It was becoming increasingly obvious that the preaching of the Gospel was chiming exactly with a widespread and deeply felt spiritual need which none of the competing philosophies of Greece, or the religions of Rome and the East, were able to come anywhere near satisfying.

Silas stayed at Antioch; and in no time at all, Barnabas and I found ourselves as fully stretched as we had ever been, preaching the Good News to a never-ending stream of enquirers, and teaching the faith in greater detail to everyone who asked to be baptised. But the team was stronger now; it was tremendously rewarding to see people I had first known as eager youngsters, maturing into wise leaders able and willing to take their places alongside the first Elders of the church in Antioch. After observing them at work, Barnabas and I felt confident enough to leave them in charge there; we agreed that we would be more usefully employed in visiting again the churches we had been able to plant on our earlier mission to southern Galatia – and that proved to be the last time we ever agreed. In all innocence, Barnabas let slip a casual remark which hit me fairly and squarely between the eyes. I forget now exactly what the remark was, but its drift was unmistakable; he was assuming that we would take Mark with us. I gazed at him open-mouthed, momentarily lost for words; then the implication of what he was saying dawned upon me, and I knew I had to be decisive. I took hold of his arm, and steered him out of the room to a quiet corner in the courtyard. "Barnabas, are you serious?" I enquired incredulously. "Are you really suggesting that we should commit the solemn responsibility of proclaiming the Gospel of Jesus Christ to a man who has broken faith with us, and left us in the lurch?" Now it was Barnabas' turn to look astounded. "I cannot believe what my ears are hearing," he spluttered. "Are you actually presuming to exclude my cousin from our ministry solely because he once turned back and went home in a perfectly understandable moment of human weakness? Coming from a man who has himself fled from danger more than once, that is quite remarkable." That was a barb that went right home. I was stung to fury, and in a moment of meanness I seized on Barnabas' reference to his relationship to Mark. "You are allowing your judgement to be warped by family considerations," I said. "You should remember what Jesus said about no one who sets his hand to the plough and then looks back being fit for the kingdom of God. Mark has done just that – how can you possibly justify taking him with us again? He is a broken reed. I cannot risk having such a man with me." Barnabas stared coolly at me. "You," he said, "appear to have forgotten what Jesus said when Peter asked him how often he should forgive someone who had done him wrong. Indeed, more than that" – his tone sharpened – "you have failed to take on board the fact that

Jesus put his own words into practice when he personally forgave Peter for denying that he ever knew him." I was angered by Barnabas' attempt to score points over me, and said so, bluntly. I could feel my gorge rising, and realised that I had better stop then, before my temper got the better of me. I stood up, imagining that that would convey an impression of dignity and authority. Unfortunately, Barnabas did so as well – and never before or since has my pride been so completely punctured by my lack of physical presence. Barnabas positively towered over me. "Then it would seem that we must part company," he said, rather portentously I thought. "I will never consent to belittling a believer, relative or not" – unnecessarily emphasising those words – "simply because he once succumbed to a loss of nerve." He turned and walked away. As I watched him go, I realised that our confrontation had not gone unnoticed – there were people standing in doorways, their faces showing their concern at what had unintentionally become a public disagreement. I bit my lip in anger at the way I had demeaned myself in front of them – and then I cursed myself for being instinctively more concerned with my own self perception, and the unfavourable image of myself I was conveying to others, than with the damage I had certainly done to the cause of Christ which I had thought I was championing.

VIII
DISCOURAGEMENT

I was ill-at-ease with myself for a long time after that. I continued to discharge my obligations within the church at Antioch; but that was what they had become – things I felt I had to do, rather than exuberant outpourings of spontaneous enthusiasm in the service of Christ, such as I had known before. Nor could I deceive myself into ignoring the consequences of my depressed mood; there was little of the pristine power which had possessed me and propelled me in the first fine flush of faith – and none of the genuine jubilant joy in Jesus which I had known at the start. I was aware that my preaching was becoming lifeless, and my teaching listless; and the realisation filled me with despair. Ineffectiveness fed upon self-preoccupation, and I found myself being sucked steadily downwards into a seemingly-irreversible vortex of depression. And my misery was only increased by my inability to pray. With the best of intentions, friends and colleagues exhorted me to pray; but try as I might, I could not generate the natural, unforced relationship with God which had me chattering away to him in earlier days like a young child to its parent. It seemed to me that I was simply going from bad to worse. In my distorted view of things I felt let down by my fellow believers; I became convinced, first that they were uncaring about me, and then that they were actually conspiring against me. I seemed to see them lurking in dark corners, whispering to each other behind their hands, furtively slipping out of sight whenever I went outside – even, occasionally, unleashing large black dogs which came menacingly towards me, teeth bared, snarling threateningly. I took to shuffling interminably round the courtyard, in the pathetic conviction that in so doing I would be able to see what was being plotted against me, and avoid being taken by surprise.

I learnt afterwards that I had been exhibiting this strange behaviour for some days, to the concern of all who shared the compound with me, when on one particularly hot summer day, in the full blaze of high noon, I became aware that the ground was rising up to meet me. I spread out my arms to embrace it, grateful to be acknowledged by something – anything. Suddenly, without any warning, there was a piercing pain in my head. It pulsed and throbbed, and drilled mercilessly into my brain. Knives flashed and lunged at me, vivid streaks of light threatened to split my mind apart, and my stomach churned and heaved with nausea. Now I found prayer forced from me involuntarily; I pleaded with God to be freed from this unbearable pain. Then I became aware that I was moving; my arms and legs jerked uncontrollably, my body shook and twitched, and I could feel my face being contorted by successive waves of spasm. There was the sound of feet running towards me, I sensed the shadows of people bending over me, and I could make out expressions of concern on faces peering down at me. "Quick, get him indoors," I heard – "gently now," as I was lifted bodily and carried swiftly into the shade of the house. A hand stroked my brow. "Get some water," someone ordered, and cold stung my face as it was splashed over me. Then I was lying on a comfortable couch, with a pillow under my head; my turban was removed, and my clothing was loosened. Through the open doorway the merest of breezes ruffled the hangings in the room; and gradually my overheated body began to sink towards a more normal temperature. I still could not bring myself to keep my eyes open; but as urgent commands and whispered questions began to subside, another sound made its low sweet way to my ears – and I realised that a little knot of believers was quietly praying in a corner of the room. Every now and then I heard words and phrases that I had so often used myself – 'Sovereign Lord', 'healing' 'Your will'; and piecemeal it slowly began to dawn on me that I had never really accepted my need of the support of others. With no wife or family to provide a network of care for me, I had developed a strategy of self-sufficiency which had not been able to meet the demands made upon it. I experienced a sudden rush of embarrassment and emotion at the realisation that I, who had hitherto been so confident in praying for others, was now myself the subject of the concentrated prayers of fellow-believers. My reaction to this discovery was astonishingly physical. Tension palpably drained out of my limbs, my body visibly subsided into a state of total relaxation, and relief flooded all over me as the intolerable pains in my head completely ebbed away. I sank into a dreamless sleep more blissful and deep than I had ever known before; and when I finally awoke, I know not how many hours, even days, later, I felt as light as a leaf drifting on a summer zephyr, as weightless as a butterfly on a delicate petal. Later, sharing with Silas the new insight into myself which this experience had given me, I was struck by the perceptiveness of a comment he made to me. "God's grace," he remarked, "is all you need; for his power is strongest when you are weak." I have hung on to that gratefully, ever since. For as I steadily regained strength, so the pressures of ordinary everyday life began again to impinge ever more directly on me. I felt a pang of regret when I learned that Barnabas had sailed for Cyprus, and that Mark had gone with him; I wondered wistfully whether we would ever meet again, and have the opportunity of repairing our ruptured relationship. But I also marvelled at God's gracious provision for me. No sooner had I lost one close colleague, than another took his place.

Silas is just about as different from Barnabas as it is possible to be. Where Barnabas is large and expansive, Silas is wiry, and slightly built. He has a thin face, with a prominent nose above a small mouth; but his eyes, deep-set and dark, hint at depths of perceptiveness to which he does not immediately admit anyone. All of a keeping with his spare physical frame, he betrays a highly-strung temperament, taut with nervous energy, crackling with creative tension; yet at the same time he is clearly in control of himself. He is an excellent listener, obviously taking in everything he hears, and mentally weighing the pros and cons of an issue before speaking his own mind on it; consequently his opinions are always worth listening to, and his suggestions more often than not turn out to be right. I had opportunities to assess his worth when we had travelled together to Antioch with the letter from the church in Jerusalem settling the controversy over Gentile believers; and without the slightest fuss or fanfare he had committed himself wholeheartedly to preaching, teaching and healing. Indeed, he became so integral a part of the team, that when his fellow envoy Barsabbas returned to Jerusalem, Silas remained at Antioch; and when I had fully recovered from the latest onslaught of illness, it was to Silas that I instinctively turned for advice and support. After his usual quiet thoughtfulness, Silas agreed that it would be wise to pick up again my earlier plan of revisiting the churches in Phrygia and Galatia, to see how they were faring. The believers in Antioch were entirely happy with the idea; and after they had commended us to the grace of the Lord, the two of us set out on foot for the hills and valleys of Cilicia.

The road took us first northward, and then westward. I was eager to make Tarsus our first objective – it had been many long years since I had been home, and almost as long since I had had any news of my parents. As gracious as ever, Silas wholeheartedly agreed; and I was surprised at how much my pulse quickened as the overlapping hills slowly unfolded as we walked, and first one, then another, remembered contour and recognised landmark, awoke responses in me. The nearer we got to Tarsus, the more I wanted to quicken our pace; but when we finally came within sight of the town, I felt a curious reluctance to cover the last few miles. Silas later told me that I had fallen unaccountably quiet and, so far from forcing the pace, as he alleged I had been doing, I suddenly held back, and needed to be urged on to complete the distance. It was mid afternoon, and very hot, when we eventually arrived. The town seemed completely deserted. Silence hung heavily in the streets – even a dog, panting in the shade of one of the little white houses, scarcely bothered to raise its head, let alone bark, as we passed. I felt an increasing sense of foreboding as we neared my parents' house. Everything was just as it had always been; but there was an air of unreality about the scene – I felt detached and disappointed, instead of eager and anticipating, as I had expected to be. Then we were at the street door. Even as I knocked, gloomy premonition weighed heavily on me. There was no answer. I knocked again. The only window was shuttered – but then so were the windows of all the other houses in the street. I was just about to knock for a third time when the shutter next door slowly opened, and a sleepy, grizzled face peered out. "Who do you expect to see there?" an old man's quavering voice enquired. "There's been no one living there these three years or more." "Why?" I asked, sharply. "What's happened to them?" "Why?" the old man echoed; "because they're both dead, that's why," and with a short inquisitive stare at me, he pulled his shutter to with the decisiveness of finality. I just stood there, stunned, gazing blankly at the only building I had ever been able to call home. Now it was that no longer. Now I had nothing – I belonged nowhere. I turned to Silas and spread my hands in a gesture of despair; but I could not see him through soundless tears. He put his arm round my shoulders, and without a word spoken we slowly retraced our steps. At the end of the street I stopped and looked back. Nothing was different – there was no movement, no sound, no sign of life at all. We were the only animate beings on the scene – and we were leaving it. There was no acknowledgement of us, no recognition of my parents in the place that had known them for the whole of their lives, no indication of any sort that they had made any kind of impact on it, nothing but unseeing, unhearing, unfeeling indifference – not hostile, not malicious, not even intentional; just completely deadening. I tried to drink in every detail of the scene, to fix it indelibly in my mind, aware that I would almost certainly never see it again; but it had no effect on me – I was emotionally paralysed, numb, unable to react to anything, to articulate anything, to feel anything. At last I slowly turned my back on the lifeless scene, and began again the weary trudge towards the west. Of course, it had to happen that our route took us past the town cemetery. I paused, and looked enquiringly at Silas. He simply nodded, and we both moved through the tombs, anxiously scanning the inscriptions; but we found nothing to relieve the dreary emptiness of bereavement, or to assuage the sudden sense of irretrievable loss. Only a single solitary goat briefly raised its head to look at us before it resumed its insatiable nibbling at the sparse vegetation struggling to survive round the bases of some of the tombs. I have never felt so keenly, before or since, the hurt of rejection, the crushing unconcern of all creation with the pain that was savaging my very entrails.

We struck out northwards, heading for the Cilician Gates. The mountains were unavoidable, so we tackled them head on. I was fairly confident for myself, for I had worked this kind of country before, when I went on my first journey with the Gospel, in the company of Barnabas; but I was initially concerned as to how Silas would cope with the demands of long journeys on foot over often challenging terrain. I need not have worried. His lean, fat-free physique was ideally suited to the conditions we encountered – and he had the advantage of me in years, as well. We very quickly settled into a steady routine, and found that our skills and aptitudes complemented each other in a way that made our journey easier than either of us had thought to anticipate. We traversed the pass without mishap, and emerged onto the wide undulating plateau of Galatia. With the inhospitable mountain range behind us, we came again into more fertile countryside. We passed scattered smallholdings, with farmers goading oxen pulling rough wooden ploughs, to prepare the soil for seeding. Then the track dropped gently down a long slow slope, and there were olive trees growing on either side. We stopped for a midday rest, and were grateful for shade from the heat of the sun. I dozed off to sleep, but was woken by the sound of sandals crunching over the hard, dry ground. A man appeared, and as soon as he found out that we were travellers, offered to bring us water. He returned with a leather bottle, and sat down to share it with us. We talked companionably. After a while he stood up, and said that he must return to his work. I asked him what he was doing. "Grafting," he replied. "We're trying to extend our stock by introducing vigorous new growth from cultivated trees onto wild ones –

there's plenty of them about," he added. We followed the gesture of his hand to the brown earth spreading away from his orderly orchard into the distant heat haze; there were grey-leaved trees, little more than shrubs, dotted about here and there as far as the eye could see. "You look puzzled," he grinned. "How do you do it?" I asked. "Come and see," he responded. We watched him select a healthy looking small branch from one of his cultivated trees. With a deft flick of a sharp-bladed knife, he made a clean diagonal cut through the branch, and took it over to one of the wild trees. After the same quick slick trick, he took the first cutting and expertly bound it with rough twine onto the cut branch of the wild tree. He had chosen his branches, and made his cuts, so skilfully, that only a slight ooze of sap through the twine gave any hint that the two parts of the branch had not originally belonged together. It was only a random incident in the course of an unremarkable day; but I found that it stuck in my mind, and the thought gradually evolved that it could be seen as a sort of acted parable of the relationship between Jewish and Gentile believers. All the fullness of the Chosen People's understanding of God was now available to those who until then had been outside his promises. I even found myself wondering if it was a picture that could be turned inside-out – could it be that God would in a sense cut back the Chosen People in order to accommodate the rest of humanity? Will he bind the two together so completely that it will ultimately be quite impossible to distinguish between them? I felt a shiver of shock at the audacity of the idea; but like the memory of the experience itself, the thought keeps presenting itself to my mind.

Silas and I pressed on. We came to Derbe. It was a genuine joy to discover that the little group of believers I had left there two years or so previously had not only survived, but had increased in numbers. We spent some days there, getting to know the new converts, and I was able to catch up with the news of the people who had come to faith during my first visit. They all seemed to be in good heart, and our visit stimulated renewed interest in the little community, with some further folk asking what it was that we were proclaiming. This was all very encouraging, and it was with high hopes that we eventually set out for Lystra. But the nearer we got to the place, the more mixed my feelings became. I still had scars from the stoning I had undergone there not so long before; and try as I might, I could not put out of my mind the picture of Jewish faces distorted by hatred, of pagan devotees enraged by the disappointment of their brief belief that the gods had come to visit them – and, most frightening of all, the patent glee with which young thugs seized the chance to hurl stones at me when I was defenceless and deserted. But I kept these personal feelings to myself, and was glad I had done so when we reached the place, and met not the slightest suggestion of antagonism from inhabitants we passed in the street, from tradesmen at their stalls in the market place, or locals peaceably passing the time of day in the town square. In no time at all we met up with people I knew from my previous stay, and again, remembered faces lit up with pleasure as they recognised me, and turned to greet Silas. We were promptly accommodated in the home of one of the believers, and a meeting was arranged for the morning of the very next day. People began arriving early, and we were introduced to those we had not met before. A line of those waiting to greet us developed; and out of the corner of my eye I caught sight of a young man, about my own height, slightly built, with thin dark hair, and high cheekbones, giving him classic good looks. Despite his youth, he had a slight stoop; but when he was introduced to me, everything about him took second place to his eyes. They were deeply-set, dark, and intense. His gaze, steady, inquiring, penetrating, seemed to embrace me with fearless frankness. As I moved to kiss his cheek, I heard someone say, clear but distant, "And this is Timothy, a third generation believer – his mother Eunice and his grandmother Lois are loyal long serving members of our congregation here…" The voice trilled on, but I heard no more words – my heart was pounding in my ears. As if in suspended time, I fought to quell a clamorous riot of conflicting emotions – I am certain my mouth opened and closed several times before I was suddenly aware that the buzz of conversation had stopped, and that everyone in the room was looking at us curiously. Timothy's face showed – what did it show? Puzzlement? Concern? I swallowed hard, and in a voice of forced naturalness said, "The Lord bless you – my son." Timothy inclined his head very slightly, and shot me one more piercing glance before moving on – and the tension of the moment broke. People started talking again; and as if detached from my body, I heard myself mumbling conventional platitudes, and mouthing appropriate clichés – but my mind was in a whirl.

I can remember very little else of that second visit to Lystra. I seem to recall that, unusually for me, I left most of the preaching and teaching to Silas. The believers in Lystra spoke highly of Timothy's spiritual perceptiveness, and his insight into the truths of the Gospel, and in all innocence suggested that both he and we would benefit if he were to accompany Silas and me on the next stage of our journey. I jumped at the idea – it would give me an undreamt of opportunity of getting to know this intriguing youth, without arousing any suspicion which might just possibly have been kindled if I had made the proposal myself. But there was a difficulty. Although Timothy's mother was a Jewess, he was presumed to be the son of a Gentile father, and as such had not been circumcised; but although my ministry was increasingly to Gentiles, I knew it would be damagingly compromised if I appeared to be countenancing, even if only indirectly, the flouting of the Jewish Law. It seemed important, as far as it lay with me, to be all things to all men, in order that the preaching of the Gospel should not be needlessly hindered; so I awaited a suitable opportunity, and cautiously broached the issue with Timothy. He asked for time to think it over; but only two days later he came to my lodging and declared himself willing to be circumcised. He took all his clothes off with unaffected unconcern; and his body's natural response to that made my task all the easier. He lay on my bed. I grasped the knife. I had not performed a circumcision before, but I had been carefully instructed how to do it, and the cutting of his foreskin was completed without a hitch. There was some bleeding, but nothing to cause concern; and in only a few days Timothy was in fine form again.

But I was not. I was totally unprepared for that encounter. All my previously submerged guilt and shame surfaced to torment me. I writhed in embarrassment as they leapt to life. They reared up in front of me, and stared at me full in the face, and gave me no respite. For a while they forced everything else out of my mind, and allowed me no rest, day or night. I struggled and wrestled to come to terms with the intractable fact that I was both an actual sinner and, despite the grace of God, still a potential sinner. For a long time I felt that my faith was fading, and that my assurance of forgiveness, which had been so confident, was failing too. All my certainty seemed to be seeping away in self-condemnation. I did my very best to conceal my inner turmoil from everyone else; but it became very much harder to maintain my self-defence when, after a short stay, we left Lystra, and moved on to Iconium. As the believers in Lystra had suggested, Timothy came with us. Inevitably, the addition of a third person to our previous two significantly altered the balance of relationships between us all – I felt that Timothy's presence was simultaneously a burden and a boon. There were, however, developments which, to my unhappily reawakened conscience, seemed to be reproaches for my past behaviour. We set out confidently enough for Iconium, and discharged our commission to tell the believers there about the decisions taken by the leaders of the Church in Jerusalem. As at Derbe and Lystra, they accepted them without demur, which was good; but I was also aware that we were so far only retracing journeys which I, at any rate, had made twice already. It was encouraging to meet, in some cases for the third time, men and women who were still holding loyally to the Way; but I was beginning to feel restless. My call had been to take the Gospel to the Gentiles; but the believers in the churches were predominantly Jewish. I felt again the need to break new ground for the faith, so it was like a breath of fresh air when, after we had moved on from Iconium to Antioch in Pisidia, we were able to turn our thoughts as to where we should go next. But the sense of release I was looking forward to, somehow just did not materialise. We had no disagreements between the three of us, there were no individual prejudices to be overcome, no group tensions needing to be resolved – indeed, the reverse was the case; we agreed that we all felt there was a barrier, invisible but very real, to our making any further progress. Pisidian Antioch is close to the frontier of the province of Asia, and I had taken it for granted that we would continue westward, and preach the Good News there. But nothing occurred to make that possible. I was, and still am, strangely unable to pinpoint any precise reason why we did not cross into Asia; but we did not because, somehow, we could not. There were no physical obstacles in our way, no political reasons inhibiting a journey to the west – it was just that when we took our bearings after leaving Antioch in

Pisidia, we discovered that we had actually travelled north-east, instead of west. We naturally made a correction to our planned route; but both the sun by day and the stars by night implacably indicated that we were now moving due north. I was privately unnerved by the irrationality of all this, but attempted to make some sense of it with the thought that we were skirting the province of Asia. Perhaps, therefore, we should revise our assumptions, and head for Bithynia; but, maddeningly, this proved to be as inaccessible to us as Asia had been. I am very conscious that all this sounds quite ridiculous, and I can no more account for it now than I could then; I can only weakly plead that this is how it was. Dark suspicions began to surface from what I recognised as the last feeble remnants of primeval chaos in my own make-up. Was I being subtly, slyly, punished for my youthful folly? Were evil forces insidiously eroding the relationship of trust in God of which I had thought myself to be so assured? The three of us talked at length and in depth in the cool moonlit evenings, and sometimes long into the cold starlit nights; and gradually the distorted perceptions I had been tempted to succumb to were shown up to be exactly that — nothing less, but nothing more. Timothy proved to be intelligent, sensitive, perceptive, with a keen mind; his slight physique belied a strength of character which I mentally marked out as likely to be of inestimable value in the service of the churches. So Silas and I took advantage of the opportunity of discussing with him what he knew of the Christian Way, and teaching him what he did not know. We encouraged him to develop and use the gifts of organisation and administration which it daily became clearer he possessed. And then, when my fever of self-doubt and depression began to subside, and I was able to replace my negative attitude to Timothy with a warm and positive appreciation of his worth and potential, the way into Asia opened up. Quite suddenly, and with no discernible explanation for the fact, we found ourselves travelling due west. We felt a surge of release and relief at this liberating development; now we were carried forward with an impetus that seemed to allow for no stopping or straying from the road – even to preach the Gospel. We knew ourselves driven by a new compulsion that quickened our pulses, lifted our spirits, and impelled us at an ever increasing pace through Mysia, direct to Troas, on the eastern shore of the Aegaean Sea.

IX
MOTIVATION

"FRESH fish for sale!..." "We'll wait for this evening's high tide..." "Three hundred denarii, then? – Done!..." "I don't like the look of the way the weather's brewing..." "Asyncritus' mother is in a poor way, you know..." "Four score bales, very best quality..." "I hear he's been posted to Alexandria..."

    We stood on the harbour wall at Troas and gaped. After weeks of walking through wild and uninhabited country, with only each other for company, Silas, Timothy and I had grown used to companionable silence. We had become attuned to the sound of the wind keening fitfully over desolate scrubland, tugging insistently at our tent flaps all night long, or singing gently in our ears as we trudged doggedly on over patchy grass and clogging sand. We had learnt to distinguish between the varying songs of birds, we could identify the calls of different animals, and we were instinctively alerted by the chilling howls of wild beasts in distant forests. But all this had been in the context of the vast silence of space, under the immense dome of the sky. Here on the waterfront at Troas our ears were assaulted by a bewildering barrage of babble, as crowds of individuals strove to communicate with each other by competing ever more loudly to make themselves heard.

There was as little silence as there was space. People thronged and swarmed, and jostled and shoved each other. I found myself half wondering whether the boys diving into the water were doing so because there was no room for them on the harbour wall – or even whether they had been pushed into doing so by the hordes of people oblivious to everything and everyone except whatever business they themselves were engaged on. And then, without warning, my head began to swim. My eyes became blurred. Within minutes, half my vision had gone. There were strong lights and jabs of pain, steadily intensifying. My stomach turned over. I lost my sense of balance, and felt myself falling, falling. Someone grabbed hold of me. I promptly threw up all over him. He let go of me, and my head cracked down on the stone pavement.

I learnt later that I had been unconscious for a night and a day. The first recollection I have is of a grave, intelligent face hovering close above me, wavering in and out of focus in rhythm with the throbbing pain pulsing through my temples. "He's regained consciousness," I heard him say. "I'll prescribe a medicinal potion for him." "Where am I?" I feebly croaked. I recognised Silas' reassuring voice – "You're in the house of Luke the doctor. He was standing right next to you when you collapsed on the harbour wall – and he is a follower of the Way!" A flood of relief surged through me, and I drifted away into sleep. Whether immediately or later, I do not know, but I began to dream – first vaguely, and then more and more vividly. Figures materialised out of swirling swathes of sea mist, outlandishly dressed. They seemed to be shrouded in flowing cloaks, with wide-brimmed hats pulled well down over their faces. They merged and parted and came together again, and slowly I was able to concentrate, until after a time I was seeing only one figure. He became more and more distinct, and loomed larger and larger. I could see that he was wearing boots, not sandals; and his feet were planted firmly on a coastline across a stretch of water. He slowly pulled his hat back from his face, and in a measured voice that resounded all around, he called out, "Come across to Macedonia and help us! Come to Macedonia! Come across and help us!" His voice trailed off, echoing eerily as it died away, leaving only a silent plea on his anxious face.

Next morning there was a brief stand-off between me and Luke. I told Silas and Timothy of the vision I had had, and announced that we would sail for Europe straightaway – that very day, if we could make a booking. Luke objected that travel was unthinkable for me for at least three days; but I sent Timothy to the quayside to find out how soon we could secure a passage. He rushed back into the house and panted that he had found a ship leaving for Philippi in two hours' time. The prospect of action worked wonders for me. I stood up, and although I felt lightheaded, I retained my balance. Luke remonstrated forcefully with me; but I was under the compulsion of a greater imperative. The other two looked at each other questioningly, but I just smiled; and without a word they set to, to roll up our bedding and baggage, and hoisted it onto their backs. Luke declared that if I insisted on travelling against his advice, he would wash his hands of any responsibility for me – then promptly changed his mind, and grumbled that he would have to come with us, to keep a professional eye upon me. By early afternoon we found ourselves leaning over the rail of a Phoenician merchantman, totally absorbed by all the bustle and activity attendant upon the departure of a ship. Then the captain shouted "Cast off!" The straining and restraining ropes holding us to the quayside splashed limply into the water, and first the harbour, then the town around it, and soon the hills behind, moved rapidly away from us, and diminished into ever-increasing distance. Every aspect of our journey had now completely turned around, from uncertainty, delay and frustration, into conviction, activity and fulfilment. Now everything seemed to come right. The memory of the recent long weary weeks of aimless wandering dissipated as promptly as the white spray flung from the bows as the ship cut a swift path through the clean green water. The sense that we were suddenly back on track in the centre of God's will was excitingly reinforced by the exhilarating speed with which we were bowled along by a stiff and steady south-easterly gale. Even the captain was surprised at how soon the island of Samothrace hove into view. We anchored there overnight, and the next day reached Neapolis in what must have been one of the fastest times ever for that voyage; and a road through a depression in the hills brought us in only a few hours to Philippi.

We took a couple of days to find our way around. I felt a certain sense of security, for although it is in Macedonia, Philippi is a very Roman city. The streets were thronged with Roman military personnel, some stationed there on duty, but many living there by choice; and a majority of the civilians were descendants of the original colonists settled there by Caesar Augustus nearly a century earlier – consequently, we heard more Latin being spoken there than Greek. Another consequence was that there was only a small Jewish community there, and no synagogue; but our landlord was a genial and expansive man, who kindly informed us that the local Jews gathered for prayers on the Sabbath at a pleasant sheltered spot on the river bank, just outside the town. So we made our way there, and sure enough, there was a little knot of people, some standing, some sitting, under the shade of the trees, while the river glided noiselessly by. Bulrushes proliferated in the shallow water at the edge of the river, thick enough to hide the nests of water birds; dragonflies hovered motionless and then darted away, only to suspend themselves again, seemingly lifeless over the placid water. Insects buzzed and hummed, now close by, now further away. Every now and then there was a quiet plop as a fish briefly broke the surface of the water and dropped back in again; and occasionally we just caught a fleeting glimpse of blue as a kingfisher dived with unerring aim and emerged with its hapless prey flapping vainly in its beak. The air was still, and the day very warm; people were conversing quietly among themselves, as if anything more than a murmur would be an unseemly intrusion into the quiet of the natural world. We approached the group respectfully, and introduced ourselves. We were welcomed graciously, and invited to contribute to the simple worship being offered there to the God of our fathers. The whole experience was profoundly calming, perfectly in tune with its tranquil setting; it was all of a piece with the pervasive presence of the river – quiet, but deep, and brimming with power. At its conclusion I was introduced to a lady named Lydia. She was neither Jewish nor European, but said that she had first been attracted to the religion of the Jews by its worship of one Supreme God, and its high moral requirements – so different from the all-too-human foibles and failings of pagan gods and goddesses. I was impressed by the earnestness of her conversation, and the perceptiveness of her insights – and also by the vibrant colour of her dress. It transpired that she was a successful business woman from Thyatira in Asia, who had built up an enviable reputation as a buyer and seller of quality textiles; apparently she had virtually cornered the local market in purple cloth. An intelligent lady, she asked some searching questions; and at the end of the day she invited us to her house to speak to her family and servants. She sat with them as we talked, clearly hanging on to every word we uttered; and yet, when she eventually declared that she believed Jesus to be the Messiah, it was quite obvious that she had not been moved by any emotional appeal – she was far too level-headed for that. Nor had she been merely convinced by rational argument – she was too warm a personality for her heart to be completely ruled by her head. I found it a very salutary experience to acknowledge that I had not converted her — I realised that the depth and strength of her commitment could only be explained as the work of the Spirit of God, bringing her to a faith so vital and vivid that it could not be described as anything less than a complete rebirth of her entire personality. The very next Sabbath we all gathered again on the quiet river bank, and without fuss or ostentation, Lydia and the members of her household entered the water, declared their faith, and emerged into new and eternal life, just as Jesus had come out of the tomb after his death and burial.

That tranquil stretch of river bank became a haven of peace during our stay in Philippi; but we were not able to enjoy it for long. Only a few weeks later we were on our way there, when a wild-eyed, dishevelled-looking girl lurched directly into our path, and just stood there, feet apart, hands on her hips, gazing intently at each of us in turn. We had no choice but to stop. At first I thought she was drunk. She began to dribble, her head started rolling about, and her eyes became unfocussed. Then I realised that she was not alone. Two men sauntered up to her, trying just too hard to look like mere curious bystanders; but the girl's reaction to them gave them away. She started when she saw them, and all the manifestations of disturbance vanished. A cold, hard glaze replaced the wildness in her eyes, and her uncontrolled limb movements subsided into constrained artificial jerks. One of the men fixed her with an intimidating stare, and in a voice dripping with odious kindness said, "Why, here are some fine gentlemen, my dear — can you tell them their fortunes?" I bristled indignantly. "There's no such thing as..." I began; but I was unaccountably stopped in mid-protest. The girl's expression had changed again. A seductive smile crept across her face. She bent forward, and moved closer towards us. Stretching out her hand, she took mine in it. "Open your hand, dearie," she murmured, in a low silken voice. I tried to pull away from her, but was startled by the strength of her grasp. "Why, sir," she said, feigning hurt, "you are a good man – why do you reject me? I see you have come from far away to bring good news to us. If you will cross my palm with silver, I will tell you how you will fare." The two men were now standing either side of her, and had transferred their menacing stare to us. Out of the corner of my eye I could see people moving towards us, curious to see what was going on. I seized the opportunity, and proclaimed in a loud voice, "We are servants of the Most High God! We announce to you how you can be saved!" The girl stood stock still, gawping at me open-mouthed. Unprompted, Silas, Timothy and Luke repeated my words in chorus, and we began to move forward. The girl's masters pulled her roughly out of our path, and we continued on our way to the riverside, accompanied now by a small crowd of people intrigued to hear more from strangers who had the temerity to stand up to powerful local racketeers.

But I soon began to wonder whether I had been wise to act in the way I did. The very next day, as we were walking through the market place, a thin high-pitched voice suddenly made itself heard above the everyday sounds of humans and animals – "These men are servants of the Most High God! They announce to us how we can be saved!" We looked at each other, but we did not need to look around – it was unmistakably the voice of the little fortune-teller. We strode on, and eventually succeeded in shaking her off; but from then on she haunted us every day, following us wherever we went in the town, endlessly repeating the words she had only too easily picked up from me. At first it was merely a mild embarrassment, but it rapidly became a serious impediment to our work. We found ourselves unable to talk to individuals, or speak to groups of people – always there was the distraction of the poor girl's demented incantation, never failing to thwart all the attempts we made to teach and preach. Her controllers were conspicuous by their absence, and I very quickly realised why – left to herself, the girl was single-handedly disrupting our mission far more effectively than anyone else could. Her unwitting persecution of us preyed on my mind. It came to dominate all my waking hours, and even invaded my dreams as well. I became obsessed with the sound of her mindless call; it rang in my ears and echoed round my brain until fact merged with fantasy, and I was worryingly unable to decide whether I was hearing it or imagining it. In the end I could stand it no more. Something within me snapped. I stopped dead in my tracks, swung round and pointed directly at the startled little figure some way behind me. Speaking to the demon possessing her, I said, "I command you in the name of Jesus Christ to come out of her." There seemed to be a brief struggle for control of her – her head, arms, legs, momentarily flailed and flapped, she foamed at the mouth and her jaw fell open, before she crumpled to the ground. She twitched convulsively, and then lay very still, white-faced and silent. As if from nowhere, her minders appeared, and lifted her to her feet. She shot me one appealing look before they propelled her away through the crowd; but I was unnerved by the baleful glare one of them directed at me before he disappeared.

In no time at all I discovered that I had good reason to be. Only two days later Silas and I left Lydia's house, where we had been lodging at her insistence since the day of her baptism. I was in the middle of remarking to Silas what a relief it was to be able to walk the streets free of intimidation, when an arm suddenly throttled my neck from behind, and another pinioned my own arms to my sides. I just caught a glimpse of the same thing happening to Silas before I was pummelled and pushed and pulled along, my feet scarcely touching the ground, until we both emerged into the main square of the town. I was aware that people were turning their heads as we were hustled along the streets; but as soon as we were thrust into the town square, it was clear that everything had been arranged beforehand. A howl of derision, obviously orchestrated, went up from a gang of ruffians strategically stationed in front of the magistrate's residence – it was no surprise at all to see the little fortune-teller's masters in the middle of the mob. It was difficult to make any sense of the ensuing hubbub – and the magistrates clearly had the same problem. Unfortunately for us, our adversaries contrived to control the whole proceedings – they shrewdly ensured the authorities' support for their scheme by accusing us of being Jews who were causing disturbances in Philippi by advocating customs which it was illegal for Romans to follow. I was shocked by the total absence of anything remotely resembling Roman legal procedures – by continually shouting and generally creating a commotion, the crowd made it impossible for the magistrates to question us, or for us to make any kind of statement in our own defence; but even that did not prepare us for what followed. We were brutally lynched. Without waiting for any authorisation from the magistrates, the mob ripped the clothes from our backs, and the magistrates, now wholly intimidated by the rioting crowd, nodded resignedly to the law enforcement officers standing by. My heart sank. Two of them moved towards each of us. I braced myself as I heard pitiless leather swish through the air; but nothing could have prepared me for the appalling shock of the metal-studded scourge tearing again and again into my bare flesh. I heard an involuntary gasp of pain from Silas; but I gritted my teeth each time I heard the fearful singing of the lash as it winged its way down on to me yet again. I do not know how many times this vicious flogging was inflicted on me; but after what seemed an eternity of unbearable agony, I was conscious of being dragged through the magistrates' residence, across a courtyard behind, and into a dark, dank airless cell. Silas was hauled in after me, our wrists and ankles were clamped into iron fetters fixed by chains to the wall, and we were left in total darkness as the heavy iron door clanged shut. We heard metallic bolts being shot home into their sockets; and then, faintly, a small child's voice – "Daddy, why are those men being shut in there?" The warder's receding footsteps echoed across the stone floor, masking whatever reply he made.

I felt myself slipping into semi-consciousness; but as I slumped forward, the unyielding manacles on my wrists and ankles cut into my arms and legs. I jerked backwards – and the excruciating impact of the raw flesh of my back on the cold damp wall behind me propelled me into full consciousness again. This happened several times, until I was eventually able to control my movements again; but full wakefulness brought with it full awareness of pain. Every nerve in my body quivered in outrage at the laceration of my back; every beat of my heart pulsed a fresh burst of pain through each gaping wound. My back throbbed; I felt burning heat and freezing cold together – and then it crept into my mind that I was not enduring anything that Jesus had not undergone. Indeed, he had suffered more than I did – I had not yet been degraded to mocking nudity, thrown callously backwards onto unyielding timber, had huge iron nails hammered hard through my shrieking flesh, then been roughly jolted upright and with pitiless cruelty dropped into a hole in the ground and left there, pinioned helplessly in blazing sunshine, as with unrelenting torture the nails slowly tore further and further into my skin and blood and nerves and sinews. The recollection of his sufferings served to put my own into perspective. I found that fixing my mind on him made me less aware of my own hurts. My thought moved on from contemplation to adoration; and as I meditated on all he had endured for love of me, I broke into spontaneous praise. There was a sudden movement in the dark beside me, and I heard Silas' voice, trembling and uncertain at first, but gaining in strength as he joined me. We came to the end of the psalm we were singing, and nearly jumped out of our skins with fright when a quavering voice suddenly called out of the darkness, "Please sing some more." Barely conscious as we had been when we were first bundled unceremoniously into the cell, we had no idea that there were other prisoners there. Now we called out who we were, and why we were there. Several different voices responded to us, and immediately the atmosphere was charged with a sense of hope. Silas and I launched gladly into another psalm of praise.

We never finished it. A deep subterranean rumble interrupted us. It gained rapidly in loudness and then, without further warning, the floor beneath us heaved and rippled, the walls all round us swayed and rocked, and large chunks of masonry crashed down from the ceiling. In one continuous frightening roar the roof fell into the cell in a cascade of tiles and timbers, the massive iron door buckled and crumpled – and when the debris finally settled and the dust began to clear, we saw the stars, glittering cool and serene in the deep velvet of the sky. After our coughing and spluttering had subsided, absolute silence reigned for a few brief seconds – then total pandemonium broke out. Dogs barked, children screamed, women shrieked, men shouted – and in our cell we discovered that the earthquake had loosened every bolt and bar detaining us. Gingerly we rose to our feet, and took a few painful steps towards each other, our chains clanking noisily as we moved. We were just beginning to make out the shadowy forms of our fellow prisoners, when a flicker of flame hurried across the courtyard. There was an audible oath, and then the sharp protest of steel being drawn from a scabbard. I realised that the jail-keeper, seeing the prison in ruins, assumed that all his charges had escaped, and was about to forestall the punishment he knew would certainly ensue, by killing himself there and then. "Do yourself no harm!" I shouted, "we are all here." The poor man fairly jumped over the rubble to get at us, and, almost incoherent with terror, managed to gibber, "What must I do to be saved?" Silas rose to the opportunity magnificently. He took the gaoler gently but convincingly from the immediate danger of which he was only too well aware, to the infinite danger from which God in Christ had made it possible for him to escape. His spiritual perception had clearly been sharpened by the frightening experience of a strong earth tremor; but the readiness with which he understood what Silas explained to him indicated that he had been steadily prepared, over years of slow maturing, for the moment of decision when the crisis broke over his head. He insisted on taking us into his house, which had not been damaged as the gaol had been; his wife bustled around to provide hot water, soothing olive oil and warm dressings for our wounds, and there and then Silas poured water over the heads of all the members of the household, and baptised them into Christian faith. With near-miraculous speed a celebration meal was produced; and we were still breaking bread and pouring wine when the first grey fingers of light began to probe the blackness of the sky.

The scene that was unveiled as dawn broke was chaotic. The earthquake must have centred on Philippi, or very near to it; and the abilities of the authorities were stretched to the limit by the need to maintain order, enforce the laws, and begin the process of clearing away rubble and repairing damage. They had clearly already decided to free themselves from the extra burden of dealing with wandering troublemakers – a messenger came from the magistrates with instructions to the gaoler to set us free. At that I dug my heels in, and made the statement we had been given no chance to make when we were arraigned on the previous day. The messenger visibly paled when I informed him that his masters bore responsibility for flogging and imprisoning Roman citizens who had not even been found guilty on any charges; and I took full advantage of my opportunity by declaring that if they wanted us out of their way, they must come in person and escort us out of the town. The messenger scuttled off, and we settled down to wait with more than a touch, I have to admit, of smug righteousness. We were not left to enjoy it for long. In no time at all, it seemed, the magistrates were at the door, and with profuse expressions of regret, but no real attempts at explanation, they accompanied us in person to the market square, and politely bade us farewell. It was really entertaining to see the reactions on the faces of the habitués of the square, as they saw the two men who only the day before had been the focus of fanatical fury, now being respectfully deferred to, and treated with every mark of esteem and honour. We made our way to Lydia's house to pick up our belongings and say our farewells; and then, to minimise the risk of her becoming an object of possibly hostile interest, we left, and took the road for Thessalonica. Luke, however, remained at Philippi, to encourage the new believers in their faith.

Our visit to Thessalonica followed much the same pattern as had emerged from our missions to other places. We went to the synagogue, and had some success in convincing a few Jews, but many more God-fearing Gentiles, that Jesus is the fulfilment of all the prophecies in Scripture about the Messiah promised by God. Intriguingly, there was again a significant number of women among the converts; but as in previous places, so in Thessalonica – the Jews who refused to believe seemed to resent even the relatively small degree of success we enjoyed there, and little more than a month after we arrived, virtually the entire city was in uproar. Word filtered through that we were to be hauled before the local magistrates, so we were smuggled out of the house where we had been lodging, and went to ground in another part of the city – and not a moment too soon. It was a frightening experience, that very night, to cower under the covers on a strange bed in an unfamiliar room, trying simultaneously to hear and to shut out the noise of the synthetic riot being artificially generated by our implacable opponents. They had stirred up the disaffected elements of the population, and harnessed the latter's anger to their own purposes; but the trouble developed its own momentum when, as we later heard, the mob besieged the house of Jason, our first host in the town. The drink-crazed crowd raised such a racket, hammering on his shuttered windows and banging on his battened door, that he was eventually driven to open the door, to appeal to them to leave him and his property in peace. That proved to be his undoing. He was instantly seized by the mob, while others rushed into the house, comprehensively ransacked it, and emerged with some other believers who had been trapped inside with Jason. They were all frogmarched to the judicial buildings, and the skilfully-led crowd were easily whipped up into intimidating the magistrates. They were shrewdly persuaded into bringing political charges, rather than racial or religious ones, which would not have cut much ice with the authorities – there was apparently much shouting about flouting the Emperor's laws, and asserting that there is a rival king, Jesus. Providentially, however, the mob did not take the law into their own hands; Jason and his associates were simply required to deposit a bond to guarantee our good behaviour, and were then dismissed. The believers persuaded us that it would be in our own best interests, as well as taking the heat off Jason and his colleagues, if we left Thessalonica; so that very night we slipped out of the city as inconspicuously as possible, and made our way to Beroea, some fifty miles distant.

Our experiences were now rapidly becoming predictable. As earlier, at Philippi and Thessalonica, so now, at Beroea, we told the Good News to the Jews, in the local synagogue; and some of them, after checking what we said with the Scriptures, declared themselves convinced. Again, a surprising number of God-fearing Gentiles also professed belief in Jesus as the Messiah; and once more I was intrigued by the fact that there were several well educated, commercially successful and socially significant business women among them. I mention the fact because it was a development neither I nor anyone else had foreseen. What we should have foreseen, however, was the hostility of orthodox Jewry to the proclamation of salvation in Jesus. We had not been long in Beroea before the by now familiar scenario unfolded of rigid traditionalists enlisting urban malcontents to make trouble for us. I reflected ruefully that fifteen or so years earlier I would have been the hottest amongst them; now I knew that the cause of the Gospel would be best served by keeping the temperature as low as possible. So when Jews from Thessalonica got wind of where we were and descended on the bemused believers in Beroea, determined to hunt us down and hound us out, I accepted that my presence could cause more trouble than the fragile new church there might be able to withstand. Once more, therefore, I set out on my travels. Silas stayed with the Beroeans, so that they were not totally bereft, and Timothy came with me. We headed south; and on a summer evening of serene beauty we came to Athens.

X
STIMULATION

THERE can scarcely be a more breathtaking sight in the whole of the civilised world. I can well believe that Rome might be grander, and I know that Jerusalem is more stirring; but for sheer beauty the palm must go to Athens. We docked at the Piraeus in mid afternoon; and by the time Timothy and I had walked the five miles or so of the road beside the ruins of the Long Walls, built five hundred years earlier to connect the city with its port, the sun was low in the west. The road at first crossed uninteresting scrubland, sparsely dotted with wild olive trees, and the occasional taller fig tree; but as we neared the city, the landscape became more attractive, with meticulously cultivated vineyards, interspersed with stands of tall cypress, dark and stately, clutching their secrets close to themselves. And then we came within sight of the city itself. Art vied with nature as we passed the ornately sculpted tombs of the famous outside the walls; but the art of death was totally overshadowed for us by the splendour of life as we caught our first heart-stopping glimpse of the hill of the Acropolis, rising majestically over the city crowded round its base, and crowned as with a diadem by the perfectly proportioned Parthenon. In the low level light of early evening, the honey coloured stone of the buildings on the summit caught and held the golden glow of the setting sun, until they briefly seemed to be almost incandescent against the deepening indigo of the eastern sky. Rarely can human skills have achieved such sublime expression – and when I eventually succeeded in lowering my gaze from the incomparable beauty above to the lower levels below, now slowly darkening into violet velvet, I was still struck by the grace and vibrancy so effortlessly conveyed in solid stone and massive marble. We passed through the city gate and made our way to the square, where we marvelled at temples and statues, public buildings and meeting places, offices and shops, images and altars, in a profusion of architectural exuberance which was nevertheless always contained and satisfying, never vulgar or overstated.

And yet, and yet – I was oppressed by a disconcerting sense of unease. I was puzzled. Why was I here? I had been irresistibly propelled out of Asia, totally unable to preach the Gospel there; but the perplexity of that experience had been clarified for me when I received such a compelling call to go over into Macedonia. All the misery of uncertainty and aimlessness had evaporated in the excitement of a new commission, and I had taken it up eagerly – only to find myself harassed and hustled and hurried by events, with less and less time to do my work in each place we visited. We had been able to stay long enough in Philippi to build up what has since proved to be a loyal and flourishing church – and at Thessalonica I was even able to get a job, and pick up my long-neglected tent-making skills again. But we had only been allowed a much shorter stay in Beroea, and now, less than a year after responding so eagerly to the summons to Macedonia, we found ourselves pushed out of the province altogether, and left to cool our heels in the alien city of Athens. What was God's purpose in allowing all this to happen?

These were the kinds of thoughts that went round and round in my mind as Timothy and I set about finding lodgings, and familiarising ourselves with the geography of the city. This was not difficult, as Athens is not large, and from wherever we found ourselves we were able to take our bearings from the splendour of the five-hundred-foot Acropolis and its temples, crowning the city with the perfection of beauty. As we walked the streets, I began to perceive a possible reason for our having been brought there. Here was I, a freeborn Roman citizen and a Jew of unimpeachable racial purity, not in Rome, the undisputed political capital of the world, nor in Jerusalem, the unchallenged religious centre of my world – but in Athens, the intellectual and cultural summit of our civilisation: Athens, whose philosophy marked the highest achievements of human thought, whose architecture influenced the built environment from the utmost east to the farthest west, and whose language was written and read, spoken and understood, by virtually the whole of the human race so far known to us. Was God, who had so clearly extended our perception of his salvation from Jews alone, to Gentiles as well, now leading us on again, creating for us an opportunity to claim the ideological powerhouse of the world as the province of the Prince of Peace? The vastness of the concept initially took my breath away; but when I regained control of my thoughts, I found myself contemplating a strategy which I had not envisaged before, but which became more and more exciting, the more I explored it. Rumour had it that Thomas was already journeying eastwards, taking the Gospel to Parthia, Persia, even India; might I not travel to the limits of the West, preaching Christ as far as Spain and the Pillars of Hercules? Was this why I had been brought so unexpectedly to the very source and centre of the all-pervasive Hellenistic civilisation of our world?

All this set my mind in a whirl of thought and prayer. If this was indeed all part and parcel of God's eternal purposes, how could it be implemented? How could it even be tested? How could it be begun? At least I recognised that the cutting short of my work in Macedonia had given me time and space in which to germinate these thoughts, and muse on how they might be developed into action. I walked the streets of Athens, wrapped in my own preoccupations and, I am ashamed to admit, virtually oblivious of Timothy faithfully at my side wherever I went, until I suddenly became aware of his touch on my arm, drawing my attention to the wealth and variety of religious devotion all around us. I was jolted sharply from contemplation of what might be, to confrontation of the here and now — and I was saddened by what I saw. Nowhere else had I seen so many altars and statues, temples and images, poignant indicators of spiritual alertness and sensitivity, almost heartbreaking evidence of a desperate anxiety to break through to the ultimate reality of life. Unparalleled effort and energy had been poured for centuries into the creation of worthy tributes to every conceivable god and goddess — even to some inconceivable ones, as well; and yet there was an unmistakable sense that these ardent Athenians, for all the integrity of their intentions, and the earnestness of their efforts, were uneasily aware that they had not achieved what they were so assiduously seeking. It was Timothy again who, remembering my poor eyesight, called me over to a small altar set in a shady bower at the intersection of two streets. He read out the inscription on it — 'To an Unknown God'. The words struck straight home, and made a powerful impression on me — they summed up exactly what I had been feeling; and they proved to be the catalyst round which my thinking was suddenly freed to crystallise. They propelled me into a burst of activity which took me from disputations with Jews and Gentile God-fearers in the city synagogue, via debates with mildly interested dilettantes in the market place, to serious discussions with passing Epicurean and Stoic philosophers who overheard snatches of what I was saying, and stayed by to hear more. Their reactions ranged from amusement to curiosity; but the whole unstructured set up was as unhelpful to them as it was unsatisfactory for me. So with civilised courtesy they invited me to make a formal presentation of my views to the prestigious Court of the Areopagus, which concerned itself with matters of religion and philosophy. It was a marvellous opportunity, and I did my best to seize it to the full. I started from their awareness of an Unknown God, and took them on to the inadequacy of any attempt to represent him in material form. Encouraged by nods of assent from people sitting on the Stoic benches, I quoted Aratus and Epimenides to reinforce my contention that God is a Person, and then moved on to proclaim that God had revealed himself in the Person of Jesus Christ, Whom he had validated by raising him from death. As always, this proved to be the critical point. Some of my audience roared with laughter; the president politely terminated the session there and then, but a few people stayed on to talk with me in depth, and ultimately became believers. And that was it. To put it bluntly, we had made no discernible impact at all on one of the world's most influential centres for the discussion of new ideas. As at Salamis on Cyprus, so now in Athens – there was no response worth the name to the most cogent case of which I was capable. I was baffled. I had rationalised our speedy ejection from Macedonia in the expectation that we were being called to claim the intellectual capital of the world for Christ; but although everything there had seemed to be in our favour, the most acute minds of our time turned from us with an indifferent shrug. Not for the first time, I was driven to reflect that opposition such as we had experienced at Philippi and Thessalonica, for example, was a better measure of the power of the Gospel to speak to people's real condition, than apathy and unconcern. I became so preoccupied with the debilitating effects of unresponsiveness, that I fell to worrying about the churches I had helped to found – after all, it is only too easy for some people to respond eagerly to a new idea, only to lose interest as soon as something else comes along, or to fall away if their new enthusiasm should entail unexpected inconvenience. More than once I floated tentative proposals to retrace our steps to Thessalonica, with the aim of encouraging the believers along the way; but as previously in Asia, so now in Achaia, something intangible but irresistible incomprehensibly thwarted my plans. In the end, torn between impatience and impotence, I asked Timothy to make the journey, to set my mind at rest. He remonstrated with me against leaving me on my own in Athens; but I insisted, and he went with good grace – I smiled to myself as I recalled the very obvious interest he and the attractive daughter of one of the influential women believers in Thessalonica had shown in each other while we were there. Again, I experienced a conflict of emotions when he left. Though I was relieved that my concern for vulnerable new believers was being met, I was surprised at how much I missed the pleasant but serious young man who had so easily slipped into a supportive, complementary relationship with me. After he had gone I mooched around Athens for a few days on my own, disconsolate, dejected, disappointed by the meagre fruit of my eager efforts. The few who had found faith were dutifully kind and supportive of me; but I had to face and accept the deflating fact that by and large, intellectual sophistication appeared to be more resistant to the appeal of the Gospel than innocent simplicity. This became unmistakably clear at my next stopping point. I took ship for Corinth – commercial, cosmopolitan, charismatic Corinth.

Timothy was not in Athens. He remained in Boerea with Silas, Acts 17:14

If Athens was impressive, then Corinth was exciting. Its buildings were not merely new – they were modern; its atmosphere ranged from the flashy to the fashionable, and its people were thrusting and assertive. They seemed to represent a microcosm of the population of the Empire – Roman officials and soldiers, Greek farmers and peasants, Syrian merchants and traders, Ionian sailors and fishermen, all jostled one another in the markets and baths, along the streets lined with shops, and in the public squares and open places. The whole city was alive with the buzz of prosperity, and the brash confidence engendered by sudden wealth. Long trains of pack animals plodded doggedly to and from each of the three harbours, laden with goods in transit between ships on either side of the narrow neck of land between the Mare Hadriaticum to the west, and the Mare Aegaean to the east. Occasionally it was not only the cargoes that were moved – entire smaller ships were sometimes hauled bodily out of the water and dragged laboriously overland on rollers, to be re-floated on the other side of the isthmus, thus saving more than two hundred miles of a hazardous voyage round the stormy southern coast of Achaia. But Corinth was also a classic example of the down-side of economic success. Situated as close as it was possible to be to the middle of the Mare Internum, it acted as a magnet to every type and condition of human existence – and there was no dominant ethos, religious, philosophical or ethical, to regulate or even influence the life of the city. An abnormally high proportion of the population was transient, and felt free to fling itself with reckless abandon into unrestrained sexual promiscuity. The streets teemed with prostitutes, and their clients' lusts were fuelled by seemingly limitless supplies of wine. I felt lonely and oppressed in this distasteful environment – but not for long. Among all the discordant groups in Corinthian society there was a surprisingly large Jewish community. Their numbers had recently been boosted by refugees from Rome, expelled by edict of the Emperor Claudius; and among them were an excellent couple whom I first met at the synagogue in Corinth. Aquila and Priscilla were 'salt-of-the-earth' people – sane, sober and sensible, honest, reliable and hard working, the very last people any ruler in his right mind would have wanted to be rid of. We related instantly. First I discovered that they were already followers of the Way; and then it emerged that they were also tent makers. Within a matter of days of arriving in Corinth as a friendless stranger, I was welcomed into the new home they had only recently found for themselves; and the three of us set about establishing a viable business as makers and repairers of tents. We put in long hours to create a credible reputation, and I was concerned by further strain on my already poor eyesight; but it did me the world of good to have fellow believers of some maturity to talk to and learn from. I followed my usual pattern of first establishing my credentials with the local Jewish community; and we had some earnest discussions in the synagogue after service on Sabbath days.

Then I had the great joy of welcoming Silas and Timothy to Corinth. Their arrival lifted my spirit, and it was good to hear the news they brought of the church at Thessalonica. At the same time, my speaking in the synagogue began to spark controversy. Aquila and Priscilla generously freed me from my share in the tent-making work, so that I could give myself full time to preaching. As a result, the temperature in the arguments I had with fellow Jews rose markedly, in inverse relationship to the quality of the debate, which sadly descended to the level of personal abuse. In the end I realised that I was getting nowhere with these intransigent die-hards; so after one particularly vituperative outburst I rose slowly to my feet, shook out the edge of my cloak, and told them that I had discharged my obligation to them, and would from now on proclaim Jesus to the Gentiles. There was a second or so of shocked silence in the synagogue; then an almighty commotion erupted. I was subjected to a deal of shouting and shoving and, reflecting with a grimace that I had been through all this several times before, I found myself pushed and pulled out of the synagogue, and dumped unceremoniously on the ground outside. Then there was an odd hiatus of uncertainty – no one seemed to know what to do next. I gratefully seized the opportunity, and with all the dignity I could muster I picked myself up, and, accompanied by a few faithful friends, moved unhurriedly to the house next door to the synagogue. It was owned by a Gentile God-fearer called Titius Justus, who had come out to see what all the fuss in the street was about. To his immense credit, he instantly grasped what was happening. "My door stands open to you, Sir," he declaimed in a clear carrying voice, "and my house is always ready to welcome you." I nodded my thanks to him, and then, on an impulse, I half turned on the top step leading into the house. I could scarcely believe the evidence of my eyes. One of the leading officers of the synagogue, a man named Crispus, emerged dramatically from the building, followed by his entire household – family, officials, servants, slaves, a veritable small procession of old and young, men and women, boys and girls. The crowd fell silent, and instinctively made way for this respected elder – and then gasped with amazement as he turned left and led his followers directly behind me into Titius Justus' house. The astonished silence of the crowd gave way to a buzz of incredulity. I was far from being the only one to sense that we had not only witnessed, but had actively participated in, a seminal moment in the history of the Way. Gentile God-fearers and full-blooded Jews had spontaneously united in a decisive demonstration of separation and identification.

exaggeration?

From now on the Synagogue of the Hebrews stood deserted, bypassed, as the Followers of the Way, whatever their origins and antecedents, pressed together into the Church of the Christians.

It was in its way a development as significant as the first unexpected response to the Gospel of Gentiles in Antioch, some fifteen years previously – and it was validated by a vision every bit as vivid as the visit of the Spirit we had all experienced on the previous occasion. Understandably, the leaders of the Jewish community in Corinth were livid at the very public humiliation inflicted on them; but they seemed to be limited to just the one mode of reaction we had now experienced in almost every place we visited – they instigated a riot against us. This time, however, I was more intrigued than intimidated. Only a few months earlier a new proconsul had arrived in Achaia; his name was Gallio, and he was a brother of the famous philosopher, Seneca. I was very interested to see how he would react to this first test of his will to rule. His judgement was paradoxically impeccable but flawed. He listened to the charge customarily made against me, to the effect that I was inducing people to worship God in ways that were against the Law. I stood up to make my defence, but he took no notice of me. He seized on the word 'law', and chose to understand it as referring to Jewish religious law, rather than Roman political law, which was certainly what my accusers had in mind. Declaring that he had no mind to be a judge of Jewish religious squabbles over words and names, he ordered his officials to clear the court, and we were all promptly hustled out of the building, prosecution and defence, witnesses and accused alike, without distinction. I scarcely had time to breathe a prayer of thanks for my delivery, when the incident suddenly turned nasty. I watched in helpless horror as, without warning, and without reason except for ugly religious prejudice, the unstable mob

Not in Acts 18:17

turned as one man upon Sosthenes, one of the elders in the synagogue who had accompanied Crispus when he so ostentatiously joined us in our house assembly. He was savagely beaten, and some brutal thugs in the gang continued viciously kicking him in the head and face, even when he fell to the ground. At that moment the standard cry went up, "Make way! Make way!" and the proconsul's self-important little procession emerged from the courthouse. I stood in open-mouthed disbelief – the attack on Sosthenes continued unabated as the representative of law and order swept haughtily by, pointedly ignoring the blatant lawlessness being perpetrated right under his disdainful hooked nose.

I was surprised at how much that incident affected me. Theoretically, I should have been vastly relieved; what started as a legal process against me had been diverted, and I had escaped – but at the cost of the totally illegal lynching of Sosthenes, a wholly innocent man. As I turned it over and over in my mind, I could not help but see it as a small, imperfect, but nevertheless telling picture of what had been done for me on the eternal scale of real, spiritual values; Jesus had borne – though, unlike Sosthenes, by his own free choice – what was justly due to me. He had suffered, and I was now free. I went to see Sosthenes. He was badly bruised, his face bloated, and his ribs sore – but miraculously, no bones were broken. He managed a rueful smile; but what touched me most was his selfless concern for my safety, rather than preoccupation with his own sufferings. "You must get away, Paul," he urged. "As soon as they've got their breath back from today's exertions, they'll realise they were cheated of their real prey – you. I fear greatly for your safety. They failed to get you by legal procedures in open court – they'll almost certainly change their tactics now, and try to do away with you in secret. You are in much more danger now than you were before today's events. Take my advice, and flee while you can." He sank back exhausted on his mat, his eyes closed, his breathing laborious. I leaned over him with a brief prayer of commendation to God, and left him with his wife and family. But his words unsettled me. I did not feel threatened; and yet perhaps I was blind to what everyone else around me could see clearly. I walked back to Crispus' house. It was night time, and I found myself the prey of all sorts of irrational fears and suspicions. There was just enough moonlight for me to imagine indistinct shapes gliding silently beside me in the shadows, disappearing unnervingly round corners of buildings, materialising threateningly where there had been no hint of a presence. I caught myself jumping nervously at tiny sounds I would normally never even have noticed; and when the wings of a bat almost brushed my face in its sudden swoop, I froze in terror. Rarely have I been so desperate to reach the safety of a building – huge relief flooded over me when the door of Crispus' house shut reassuringly behind me. Fortunately, everyone except Crispus had gone to bed, and I did not have to make a prolonged pretence of feeling unconcerned. A brief exchange of the customary courtesies freed me to make my way to the guest room; but sleep eluded me. All my senses had been sharpened by the imagined threats of my late-night walk, and I lay wide awake. My eyes could not resist the pull of the pool of moonlight thrown on the floor from the small window high up in the wall. I gazed intently at it, fascinated by the strength of the attraction it exerted on me. I heard the click of the wooden latch as Crispus closed his bedroom door; and then utter silence reigned. So far from gliding into sleep, I was elevated to a new height of consciousness. My sensitivities seemed to be acutely tuned. I felt in full control of myself, but at the same time wholly controlled by something – Someone – outside of myself. All my powers gathered into an ecstasy of total concentration –

and then the Lord was standing there, white in the moonlight, as real as the darkness all around. Trembling with awe, I rose to my knees; but I got no further. "Have no fear," he said; "go on with your preaching and do not be silenced, for I am with you and you will not be harmed by anyone's attacks. There are many in this city who are My people."

And so it turned out. Hostility to us and our message subsided as unexpectedly as it had erupted, and I enjoyed a freedom to preach in Corinth which I had not known elsewhere. It was matched by a comparable willingness on the part of my hearers to listen and respond – no doubt due in part to the fact that the population of the city, placed as it was at a meeting point of trade routes from east and west, were more open to new ideas than people in provincial inland towns. This had its down-side as well, though. I rapidly discovered that Corinthian morals were extremely lax, and sat ill with the values and standards which were the very warp and woof of my own strict upbringing. I early found myself battling to prevent the Lord's Supper from degenerating into the kind of drunken orgy which all too often characterised a Corinthian love feast; and the church seemed to be genuinely baffled by my condemnation of a member who was openly flaunting his relationship with his stepmother. The unbelievers seized gleefully on this aberration when they heard about it, unctuously proclaiming their moral superiority to the Christians – I was deeply saddened by the damage this 'incident' did to the church. But there were successes as well as failures, and though most of the converts were ordinary people, we were glad to welcome also the City Treasurer, Erastus – he had marked his period in office by paying out of his own pocket for a stretch of pavement to be laid in front of the theatre. Busy but happy days succeeded each other so rapidly, that a year and a half passed before I began to feel again the need to revisit churches already in existence, to see how they were progressing, and to encourage them in the faith. I was delighted when Aquila and Priscilla offered to come with me – they had proved firm friends all the time I had been in Corinth, sound advisors when I needed help with pressing problems, and sympathetic listeners when I had to share with someone else the tensions generated by misunderstanding and opposition. But it was with a real pang of sadness that I paused at the turn in the road which finally took us out of sight of Corinth, for one last, long lingering look at the tumultuous but lively city which had given me such a prolonged opportunity for preaching the Gospel of the Grace of God.

XI
REACTION

visited Oct. 2002

"BY the way, do you know of a reputable barber anywhere? I have made a solemn vow, and I wish to commit myself to it publicly by having my hair cut off." Aquila, Priscilla and I were approaching Cenchraea, where we planned to take ship for Syria, and it occurred to me that this could well be the last opportunity I might have of undergoing such a rite before seeing again the believers I hoped to visit. "Well," drawled Aquila, with a half amused *fiction!* sidelong glance at me, "I don't know of one on this particular road – but I do know Phoebe, who lives at Cenchraea, and she may well be able to help you. What is more, she is a follower of the Way; I shall be delighted to introduce you to her." All worked out as he had expected. It even transpired that the church at Cenchraea met in Phoebe's house, so I had the opportunity of meeting another group of fellow believers – and my admittedly sparse locks were duly culled.

Down at the harbour there was no news of a sailing for Syria in the reasonably near future, so we had to settle for what was available. We booked a passage for three to Asia, and after a trouble-free voyage to the mouth of the River Cayster, we continued on foot to Ephesus. Here my two very good friends had business leads to follow up, so we parted company. I had at this stage no contacts in this big and busy city, so on my first Sabbath day there I made my way to the synagogue; but rather discouragingly, I experienced no compulsion to proclaim Jesus there. I was received politely enough, but I felt that I was doing little more than following a humdrum routine when I spoke – I knew there was no real drive and conviction in what I said. I reflected ironically that I was usually driven out of the synagogue when I preached with passion; at Ephesus, where all was calm and sweet reason, I was asked to stay longer. But I knew I was not impelled by the Spirit, so I declined their kind invitation as gracefully as I could, and attempted to salve my own conscience by promising to visit them again if the opportunity presented itself.

What I discovered, though, was that it was not possible to 'salve my own conscience' – at least, not by mere activity. I followed through the plans I had provisionally projected: from Ephesus I travelled back to the coast, took passage for Caesarea, journeyed up to Jerusalem to report to the church there on what I had been doing, and finally returned to Antioch after three years' absence. But there was little sense of achievement, precious little feeling of fulfilment, even, I rather resentfully thought, any adequate appreciation of all I had been through in the cause of the Gospel. When I stood back and took stock of this period of deflation, I wondered if the reason for it lay within me, or outside of me. For almost all the time I had been away, I had been in the company of other people, who checked me and encouraged me, stimulated and stretched me, gave me pause for thought and impetus for action. Then circumstances had conspired to leave me on my own for several months, and I felt the contrast – perhaps all the more keenly because I had no way of knowing that it was coming, and preparing myself for it. I learnt that I was bad company for myself, and that I reacted adversely when thrown back on my own resources. Ultimately, it proved to be a salutary period in my life. I emerged from it aware of weaknesses in my character which I had not previously known of, and the knowledge spurred me on to make a conscious effort to overcome those weaknesses – most importantly of all, <u>to seek the Lord's help</u> in bringing my personality disorders under his healing control. I resolved there and then to be content with whatever circumstances I might find myself in.

Maybe I was too smug, too satisfied with my own selfrighteousness in having made such an eminently praiseworthy decision – but it was immediately tested, and tested sorely. There was a sudden commotion at the street door one afternoon – shouts of surprise, shrieks of delight, exclamations of welcome – and in walked Peter. I had of course seen him quite recently, in Jerusalem; but he had said nothing then about coming to Antioch, so I was as surprised as anyone else by his visit. I was delighted to see him, and he greeted me warmly; but I was naturally curious as to why he had come, and could only conclude that he had decided to investigate, possibly for himself, but more likely on behalf of all the leaders of the church in Jerusalem, exactly how the Jewish/Gentile mixed church in Antioch was developing. But there was not the slightest hint of suspicion about the motive for Peter's visit; he mixed freely and unaffectedly with the whole fellowship, was affable and encouraging to everyone without exception, and joined us without a qualm when we all ate together. So I was more than a little surprised when, only a few days later, we received another group of visitors from the Jerusalem church – surprised, because their coming had a strange effect on Peter. He was clearly taken aback by their arrival, and appeared to be agitated by it, as well. There was a slight but noticeable change in his attitude

See Galatians 2:11 sq.

to the Gentile believers in the fellowship – he was just that little bit less open and friendly with them. I was disturbed by this; and then the time came round for the weekly fellowship meal which all the believers shared in on each Lord's Day. I was saddened to see the party from Jerusalem pointedly moving one of the tables away from contact with any of the others in the room; but I was angered when Peter went and reclined with them there. I brooded darkly over his barefaced duplicity. I could feel my blood rising as I watched him smiling and conversing so pleasantly – but only with Jewish Christians. My disgust with his deceitfulness completely ruined my own appetite; and in a move which I admit surprised me as much as anyone else in the room, I suddenly pushed my plate away from me, stood up, and in the stunned silence that descended on the gathering, I publicly berated Peter for having double standards. I was enraged by his refusal to eat with Gentile Christians when Jewish believers were present, though he had happily done so before the latter arrived. I realised immediately that I had made a mistake; I was right to be offended by Peter's shameful attitude, but wrong to have acted in the way I did. In the buzz of consternation that ensued, I went over to Peter and apologised for overreacting; and he in his turn acknowledged that his own behaviour had been less than honourable. The relationship between us was restored; but I was humbled by the ease with which my temper had got the better of me. I realised that I had lost some of the confidence and respect I had won from the church at Antioch over the years, and I had perforce to accept that it would take time to eradicate the memory and the effect of my sub-Christian outburst from the minds of the believers who had witnessed it; so I decided to stay at Antioch for quite some time, working at rebuilding old friendships, and making new acquaintances. But I became increasingly convinced that I ought to visit once more the congregations of believers which had resulted from my first journey through Asia with Barnabas, all those years earlier. This time, however, I travelled on my own – but with none of the dejection and flatness of spirit which had plagued me on my last journey. Now I was buoyed up by the challenge of rivers to cross, bandits to avoid, days without food and nights without sleep; and by the anticipation of meeting again with highly regarded Christian leaders and their faithful followers. Their enthusiasm and encouragement was a big help in carrying me through the inevitable problems I encountered in the churches. There were people who had grasped the Good News imperfectly, and were unwittingly leading their fellowships into error. There were others, more dangerous because more determined, who saw in these new groups of freely associating, earnest religious people an unexpected opportunity to advance themselves to positions of leadership, in which they could manipulate the gullible to their own advantage. It proved worryingly difficult to convince some of these churches that they were in danger of falling away from the Gospel which had first brought them into being. As I journeyed again through Galatia and Phrygia and Asia, I sensed a growing tendency to regard knowledge as the route to salvation, instead of faith in Jesus. This trust in intellectualism was, I found, evolving into fantastic theories of hierarchies of revelation, in which self-designated 'experts' claimed spiritual superiority over mere initiates. In other instances, the glorious freedom of grace, the undeserved kindness of God, was being perverted into uninhibited licentiousness – indeed, I discovered to my horror that some deluded souls were actually advocating unrestrained sinning in order, so they argued, that God's glory might be further enhanced by increasing the extent of his forgiveness. Contact with these developments forced me to think of ways of combating them. Faced with the impossibility of being in more than one place at one time, I realised that I must put into writing the facts I had received, both from the first apostles and eyewitnesses of the Lord Jesus, and directly from the Lord himself. The concept of letters to the churches began to form in my mind – first, of letters to individual churches on specific issues raised by them, or on matters on which they needed guidance; and then of more general teaching letters, which could be circulated to groups of churches within reasonable distance of each other.

But no sooner had the idea formed in my mind, than it had to be shelved under pressure from more immediately demanding circumstances. I came to Ephesus, in fulfilment of my earlier promise to visit again if I could. There I had a very welcome surprise – I found a small but keen Christian community which, to my even greater delight, I discovered owed much to the loyal labours of my old friends Aquila and Priscilla. They had been a great help to a believer called Apollos, who had come to Ephesus from Alexandria; he was apparently very well grounded in the Scriptures, and was a convincing teacher of the facts about Jesus, but the only baptism he knew about was John's. I discovered this for myself when talking to a group of about a dozen believers one day. I asked them if they had received the Holy Spirit when they were baptised, and was somewhat taken aback when they said that they had not even heard of the Holy Spirit; but they were eager to learn, so I took them on one side and explained how baptism in the Name of Jesus went a lot further than the baptism John had administered. They asked some searching questions, and then fell very quiet. As so often before, a profound silence filled the room. I knew, and I knew that they knew too, that the Spirit of God was filling our hearts and minds, purging our emotions and intellects, and irresistibly commanding our intentions and wills. We waited long in solemn submission to the sublime sense of the presence of the Living Jesus, perceptibly intensifying through all the space we occupied, all the time we were there, until, knowing myself to be impelled by the Lord himself, I rose, and in the Name of Christ laid my hands on the head of each man in turn. As I moved from one to the next, a murmur of worship broke and continued; and I realised to my surprise that by the end I was hearing the praise of God being sounded out in twelve different living languages.

I had not the faintest idea what my next move should be; but neither did I have the faintest disquiet about the fact. As it turned out, a familiar pattern of development emerged. Acting, as I believed, in obedience to my first obligation, I attended the synagogue in Ephesus for at least three months; but the more impassioned my advocacy of Jesus as the Messiah, the more malignant became the hostility of the self-appointed guardians of Jewish orthodoxy. As earlier in Corinth, so now in Ephesus, I left the synagogue. This time I took a lease on a lecture hall, and a steady stream of people came and went, listening to the preaching and teaching of the Way, asking questions, discussing problems, arguing among themselves – I had to renew the lease several times to accommodate the continuing flow of interested enquirers, and eventually it extended to a full two years' tenancy. This was all very encouraging; but at the same time elements began to emerge about which I was less happy. *Acts 19:11* A craze unaccountably developed for borrowing articles of my clothing. I discovered that they were being taken to sick people, for them to touch; but although there were authenticated instances of healing having taken place by these means, I could see that the faith in the name of Jesus with which this tendency had originated, would rapidly degenerate into an assumption of mechanical efficacy in the items themselves – a perversion which would do a great deal more harm than good. One day there was another less than helpful phenomenon associated with us. A noisy hullabaloo suddenly erupted in the street outside the lecture hall. We all rushed out to see what it was about, to be greeted with the spectacle of no fewer than seven stark naked men leaping about all over the place, howling and hollering, trying to escape the frenzied fury of an eighth man who was laying about him with a huge cudgel, thrashing each and every one of them with the strength of the demented – and drawing blood in the process. It turned out that the unfortunate victims had been claiming to cast out evil spirits 'in the Name of Jesus Whom Paul preaches'. Their demon-possessed tormentor had apparently growled that he knew of Jesus and he knew of Paul – but he had never heard of these seven sons of Sceva, and in an unrestrained outburst of irrational rage, he had lashed out at the wholly unsuspecting charlatans, and succeeded in putting them all to embarrassed flight.

The incident was judged to be a vindication of our work and witness; but I had private misgivings – this was not the image of the Way that I had received, nor one that I was happy to see propagated. I let my feelings be known, and almost predictably there was then what I considered to be an overreaction. One of the believers who had previously practised sorcery asked Tyrannus, the landlord of the lecture hall, if he could make a bonfire of his paraphernalia in the courtyard. Tyrannus raised no objections, so the fellow went ahead. The idea caught on like, inevitably, wildfire. People rushed to join what seemed at first to be a high-minded act of renunciation; but the whole thing rapidly got out of hand. Scrolls full of spells, witches' wands, bells and baubles, candles, incense, bizarre headgear and outlandish vestments – my eyes fairly popped out of my head at the number and variety of the articles by means of which these superstitious people had been seduced into subjection to evil spirits. It was certainly exhilarating to watch this mass renunciation of the symbols of enslavement – but exhilaration turned to increasing alarm as the bonfire was recklessly augmented by irresponsible bystanders. Clouds of smoke billowed into the dark night sky, and showers of sparks sprayed in all directions as hungry flames leapt higher and higher. It was only Tyrannus' prompt action in organising a team of volunteers to fill buckets of water from the nearby well and to throw them, not on the fire, where they would have been totally ineffective, but on the buildings of the courtyard all round it, that saved his lecture hall from destruction. How close it had come to catching alight only became apparent next morning, when he pointed out to me blackened plaster and charred timbers, some of them still smoking, and far too hot to touch. I found myself wondering whether excitability was a dominant characteristic of the west Asian temperament.

[margin note: *Imagination!*]

I very soon had even more reason to suspect that it was. Tyrannus understandably declined to renew my tenancy of his lecture hall when it next came up for renewal; but I did not regard this as in any way a blow – after two years' fruitful work in Ephesus, I was beginning to feel again the prompting of the Spirit to travel. I made mental plans to go west to Macedonia, south to Achaia, and then south-east to Jerusalem. In the longer term I still wanted very much to travel to Rome – and always at the back of my mind the thought of Spain in the far west continued to tug at my hopes and aspirations. I got as far as sending Timothy and Erastus ahead of me to Macedonia – and then Ephesian volatility threw everything into turmoil.

Two years' work had produced converts in Ephesus; but, inevitably, it had also generated controversy. The progress of the Gospel had begun to make a small impact on the sale of little silver images of Artemis, the local goddess; but the incident of the bonfire of the sorceries had apparently sent sales into a steep decline, and the local guild of master silversmiths decided to act. Their convenor, Demetrius, called a meeting, at which he early slipped in a passing reference to their falling incomes, the blame for which he laid fairly and squarely on my shoulders, mentioning me by name. Then he demonstrated the deft touch of a demagogue by dwelling heavily on the dishonour done in this way to Artemis and, by association, to the whole province of Asia, where her worship was widespread, and to their own city of Ephesus, the jealous guardian of her temple. This much I heard from Gaius, one of the believers, who had found himself on the edge of the crowd at the meeting, and had listened with growing consternation until Demetrius' oratory succeeded in whipping up his hearers into a mindless frenzy. Even as Gaius was breathlessly pouring out his report to me, I could hear the hubbub of shouting in the distance. Gaius insisted on returning to the scene, in order to keep me up-to-date with developments. Sensing real danger, I forbade him to go; but Aristarchus said he would go with him, to ensure his safety. The next thing I heard was that they had both been recognised as followers of the Way, had been seized by the near rioting mob, and were being hustled roughly through the streets to the amphitheatre. I was now seriously alarmed. Everyone knew that wild animals were kept in a state of near starvation at the amphitheatre; if the crowd got completely out of control, hotheads among them could encourage them to overcome the keepers, open the cages, and let the ravenous beasts loose on the two defenceless Christians. Completely ignoring the pleas of the other believers, I set out for the amphitheatre, determined to do whatever might be needed to save my two friends. I was amazed, and at first angry, to find myself physically restrained by some of the men in our group; but infuriating though it was, I had eventually to agree that my appearance in front of the frantic crowd would probably only have made matters worse for the two virtual hostages. It rapidly became obvious that, like the enthusiastic incendiaries of only a few nights previously, Demetrius and his colleagues had started something they could not control. From the flat roof of my lodging house I could see the amphitheatre, fairly heaving with countless thousands of agitated creatures, for all the world as angry as an ant hill disturbed on a hot summer afternoon. But there the analogy ended – no ant hill ever made anything remotely approaching the noise coming that day from the amphitheatre of Ephesus. An indescribable roar was splitting the air, shattering itself on the tiers of seats rising all around, and running back together again, like angry waves of the sea frustrated in their assault on a cliff face, thrown back, only to clash with the inexorable advance surging in behind. It was a terrifying demonstration of how thin is the veneer of law abiding civilisation on which we so confidently build. A few unscrupulous rabble-rousers had unleashed a beast which in no time at all ripped completely out of their hands, and spread with appalling speed, utterly swamping any vestiges of rationality in the individuals making up the crowd. We heard afterwards that the vast majority of the people in the amphitheatre had no idea at all why they were there, or what the hubbub was all about – they had simply been swept off their feet by the dynamic of an excited crowd submerging their individual judgements, whether willingly or not, in the mindless will of the massed mob.

But if the confused crowd was frightening, the controlled crowd was terrifying. Our Jewish opponents made a desperate attempt to seize direction of the riot for their own purposes. They propelled a man called Alexander to the centre of the stage. He started confidently enough by making gestures to quieten the vast concourse of people, and seemed to be on the point of succeeding in making himself heard, when someone bawled out, "He's a Jew!" Instantly all pandemonium broke out again. A great roar of scorn and derision promptly put paid to any hope the unfortunate Alexander might have had of influencing the mob. From somewhere in the stadium a chant began – "Great is Artemis of the Ephesians!" It was immediately taken up all round the amphitheatre; and the crowd which was frightening enough when it had no common purpose uniting it, now became chillingly terrifying as it was suddenly transformed into a monstrous unity, with one single dominating motive. The vast mass of humanity was gripped by a corporate insanity, as for two solid hours virtually the entire population of Ephesus drove themselves into a state of intoxicated madness with their inanely repeated chant. It seemed as if nothing and nobody could break their self-induced hypnosis; but at long last, as the ardour of the blazing sun began to cool, exhausted individuals started to sit down, and the noise level gradually dropped. Ultimately it was the town clerk who finally succeeded in asserting his authority as the representative of law and order. The enormous gathering slowly fell silent as he began cautiously enough by agreeing with them about the greatness of their goddess; then having thus skilfully won their confidence, he became bolder, and moved on to scolding them for their lawless behaviour. Whether or not his hearers realised it, he actually made a defence for us and our activities; and by the time he came to warning them that their conduct that day might well lay the whole city open to a charge of riot and civil commotion, he had his entire audience hanging on his every word. With consummate skill he dismissed the assembly at exactly the right moment, neither risking a renewal of the disturbance by letting them go too soon, nor losing his influence over them by detaining them too long. In sheepish submission, the many-headed monster separated out into weary and embarrassed individuals, filing in orderly fashion out of the huge amphitheatre, and dutifully dividing into the darkening city streets.

A couple of days later I judged that the whole upheaval had subsided to the point where it was safe for me to go ahead with my plans for revisiting Macedonia, and then Achaia. After three months there, I was on the point of embarking for Syria, when yet another Jewish plot against me surfaced; so I travelled back to Macedonia, utilising to the full the unexpected opportunity of meeting again the Christian believers in the churches there. I enjoyed the company of seven colleagues for part of the way; but they went on ahead to Troas, while I met up again with Luke at Philippi. All nine of us then stayed for a week at Troas. Our last day there was the first day of the week, so we met with the fellowship for the breaking of bread. I was now beginning to appreciate that I would not be able to keep on revisiting each church, so I wanted to take advantage of every opportunity of teaching them as much as I could. The believers at Troas agreed to meet again when the day's work was ended; and we assembled in their usual meeting place, on the third floor of a town centre building. The night was warm, the room was full, and a lot of oil lamps had been lit. I was wholly taken up with what I was saying, and hardly noticed how stuffy the atmosphere had become. I suppose I noticed that a few people's eyes were glazing over; but I was totally unprepared for what happened just before midnight. There was a half-stifled yell, and young Eutychus, who had been perched on one of the window sills, fell backwards out of the window and landed with a stomach-churning thud on the street three floors below. There was a horrified shriek in the room. I joined the rush for the door, and as I stumbled down the stairs, not knowing what to expect, Elijah and Elisha both unaccountably flashed across my mind. They had both, I remembered,

155

restored young men to life by stretching themselves full length on their dead bodies; and as soon as I reached the street I knew why I had been prompted in that way. Eutychus' distraught mother was already keening inconsolably, cradling her dead son in her arms. She looked at me imploringly, and yielded the teenager to me without a word. I breathed a silent plea to God, and embraced the young man as he lay there on the ground. The God of Elijah and of Elisha and of Jesus revealed his mighty power again, and graciously restored Eutychus to life. We all slowly reclimbed the stairs, and broke bread together again in a profoundly moving renewal of our earlier Eucharist of Thanksgiving.

After my recent experience at Ephesus I thought it wiser not to call there again so soon – in any case, I was keen to be in Jerusalem by the day of Pentecost; so I embarked at Assos, and after three days' sailing landed at Miletus, where I invited the elders of the church at Ephesus to meet me. It was a hard occasion. I instinctively knew that it would be the last time I would see them, and I told them so. As at Troas, I felt an urgent need to impart to these church leaders all I could in the short time available to me, because from then on they would be the only guides and mentors of what was still a young and relatively immature church; but it was far from being merely a one way encounter. They had questions for me to answer as far as I was able, and opinions and points of view for me to comment on where appropriate. In the privacy of our meeting room we all knelt in prayer and commended each other to the grace of God; but we made our farewells in full view of the good people of Miletus, as we kissed and embraced on the quayside immediately before boarding ship for the next stage of our much-interrupted voyage. There were many open mouths and raised eyebrows among the local folk round the harbour that day; and among us, few dry eyes as hawsers were slipped, the anchor weighed, sails unfurled, and clear water put between us and the land.

Slowly but steadily, Kos, Rhodes, Patara and Cyprus loomed ahead one after the other and sank away astern as we kept to an east-by-south-east course, until eventually the impressive city of Tyre emerged out of coastal mist, and we made landfall in Syro-Phoenicia. When we met the believers in Tyre I felt a sudden elation that the followers of the Lord, the new Israel of God, were already to be found in so many places around the Great Sea, and so widely dispersed throughout the Empire of the Romans. When we left the believers in Tyre, I experienced a leaden apprehension as to what the future might hold – throughout the whole of our week's stay with them they had pleaded with me not to go on to Jerusalem. In Miletus we had prayed for each other in private; but the Christians in Tyre proved to be considerably more extrovert – when we insisted on leaving, the whole church accompanied us down to the beach, where we held an impromptu prayer meeting. I was conscious of being under steadily increasing pressure to abandon my plan to visit Jerusalem, and I was perplexed by it – was it the guidance of the Lord the Spirit, or was it a test of my commitment to my mission? I decided that the only way of finding out was to continue with my plan until it was made impossible, by whatever means, for me to go any further with it. So we pressed on to Caesarea, where we found lodging with Philip, who had been a colleague of young Stephen all those years ago, when the Apostles had appointed the first seven Deacons to serve the infant church in Jerusalem. The signs became clearer, and distinctly less encouraging. Philip's house in Caesarea seemed to be taking on the nature of a staging-post for itinerant Christians – while we were still there, he took in a lodger by the name of Agabus. Agabus was taut, tense, taciturn. His piercing eyes set deep within his gaunt face seemed to penetrate, rather than merely fix, the object of his gaze. With his rough, animal skin coat, thin legs and bare feet, he immediately put me in mind of all I had ever heard about the appearance of John the Baptist. There were occasional moments when he dropped his guard sufficiently to talk briefly with us; but he spent much of his time sitting cross-legged on the ground, his eyes closed, his back as straight as a rod, slight movements of his straggly grey beard the only indication of intense internal verbalisation as he opened himself to the Spirit of God. It was in the course of just such an ecstatic experience one day that Agabus suddenly opened his eyes, turned his head to look directly at me, and without for one second relinquishing his imperious visual hold of me, rose unhurriedly to his feet and came towards me. Distant and impersonal, he slowly unfastened my belt, and resumed his meditation position. Everyone else in the room watched with fascination as he deliberately and expertly tied his own hands and feet together, with my belt. Then, after a long pause, he finally spoke. "These are the words of the Holy Spirit. Thus will the Jews in Jerusalem bind the man to whom this belt belongs, and hand him over to the Gentiles." It was the longest sentence any of us had heard him utter. We were all spellbound. After a while he calmly freed himself, stood up again, and gave me back my belt. With never another word spoken, he left the room; and none of us ever saw him again.

I know the brothers and sisters meant well; but to the blood-chilling fear which Agabus had induced in me, they now added the mental anguish of decision and the emotional weight of loneliness. I was harried from all sides with heartfelt pleas to drop my determination to go to Jerusalem; and this time there was no external encouragement from the Lord Jesus, no clear direction as to what I should do, no nocturnal vision to stiffen my resolve. I was thrown back entirely on my own powers of deliberation, decision and determination. I have rarely felt so alone in all my life, either before or since.

XII

DANGER

"PAUL! Why, it's good to see you again! How are you? However many years is it since we last met? Do you know, you've hardly changed a bit – well, not so much that I wouldn't have recognised you straightaway, anyhow! Come on in, and welcome. You must be exhausted after such a long journey. Sit down while I get water to wash your feet, and then we'll have a meal. There's so much to talk about, isn't there, but I promise you we'll take our time over it – we must not tire you out before you've had time to get your breath back, must we?" Despite my weariness, I smiled spontaneously, and felt some of my tension drain away as Mnason and I embraced and greeted each other. "Well, my good old friend," I grinned, "you haven't changed, either." Neither had he. Mnason, I was relieved to discover, was still the same voluble, cheerful, outgoing character I had got to know in my very first days of faith. He had been introduced to me by Barnabas – like him, Mnason was a Cypriot – when Barnabas so generously sponsored me as a genuine believer on my first visit to Jerusalem after my conversion. And now here I was, in Jerusalem again, and lodging with a man who had held the faith through thick and thin, in season and out of season. His welcome was so warm and sincere that I felt I had as good as come home. "Right, so what are your plans now?" Mnason's wife placed dish after dish of tempting food on the table, and we talked long into the night. "Well, I would dearly love to meet James again, and all the other leaders here in Jerusalem," I replied. "Of course," Mnason said, "we'll do that tomorrow – I mean today," he corrected himself with a chuckle. "If we don't let you get to bed now, you'll be in no fit state to meet anybody in the morning." He showed me to their little guest room, with only a simple bed on the floor; but I was sound asleep almost before my head hit the pillow.

Next morning I was woken by the reassuring sounds of ordinary everyday city life getting under way again – outside my window, the low rise and fall of voices in conversation, sandals slapping on stones, snatches of bird song, the mild protests of animals being goaded along the street, and occasional shouts from traders hawking their wares; inside the house, intermittent talk, water being poured, the clink of bowls and pans and dishes being washed and stacked and used again. For a while I lay and listened, content with the security of obscurity; but then, as my faculties came into full focus, my mood darkened. I was, once again, in Jerusalem – and I remembered that I had received three distinct warnings about trouble in Jerusalem. I could not help feeling apprehensive – when would it come? What form would it take? I reflected that knowing that trouble was certain, without knowing any of its details, was more unnerving than meeting it unexpectedly. But it didn't come that day – there was a warm reunion with James and the other leaders of the church, and the added lift of hearing that thousands of Jews had become believers. Looking back on that meeting later, it dawned on me that it was then that the merest hint of a shadow of what was to come first flitted briefly over me. James suggested that in order to disperse any suspicion among ardent upholders of the Law that I was undermining it, I should join four other men who were about to undergo a purification rite – and he pointedly added that my action would carry even more conviction if I were to meet the expenses of the rite for the other four, as well as for myself! I grinned and agreed, and went ahead with the ritual, duly giving the required seven days' notice of completion of the period of purification; but the long forecast storm suddenly broke over my head, without any warning whatsoever, one day short of the completion of my vow.

I was walking on my own through the Temple precincts when a gang of Asian Jews suddenly emerged from behind a cluster of pillars. Before I could react in any way I was totally surrounded, and subjected to a hail of blows from fists and feet. In no time at all I was the helpless centre of a seething mass of humanity, as people came running from all directions, shouting and shoving and sweeping me off my feet. The mob generated uncontrollable momentum, and I broke out in a cold sweat as I heard the massive bronze doors of the Temple clang ominously together – now I was outside the limits of sanctuary, and my attackers could throw the last vestiges of conventional restraint to the winds. With less and less success I tried to ward off the vicious thumps and kicks raining down upon me. I remember wondering, in a fleeting flash of absurd reasoning, whether I was being attacked for the money I had brought to Jerusalem for the relief of the poverty stricken Christians there; believers in Asia, Macedonia and Achaia had collected a substantial sum for them, and word would inevitably have got around that I had been entrusted with delivering it. Then, suddenly, the beating stopped, and the hubbub subsided. I guessed why. The crowd parted, and I was surrounded by a detachment of Roman soldiers. They pulled me roughly to my feet, and I was promptly loaded with two heavy iron chains. The commander started to ask me who I was, and what I had done. Uproar broke out all over again. The hapless officer could get no sense from anyone, so he ordered his men to take me into the barracks. Enraged that they seemed to be on the point of losing their prey, the mob surged forward – had it not been for the armed troops encircling me, my life would certainly have ended there and then; but the soldiers lifted me bodily up the steps into the fortress, to the fury of my frustrated foes. I asked the commander, in Greek, for permission to speak before being taken inside – and it emerged that he had assumed that I was an Egyptian terrorist leader who had caused trouble some time previously. I cleared up that little misunderstanding, and from the top of the steps turned to face my persecutors.

The strong gold light of the late afternoon sun picked out in sharp detail every facet of the scene before me. The elegant white columns of the portico surrounding the courtyard glistened with pristine clarity, and the colours painted on their ornately carved capitals glowed with the brilliance of newly completed artistry. Beyond, varied shades of white and beige and red jostled with each other in an unregulated riot of colour as the houses of the city seemed to pile on top of one another in crazy confusion; and then, serenely crowning all the apparent disorder crowding around it, the incredible glory of the Temple, almost unbearable to look at, as its golden roof sparkled and flashed in the rays of the sun – and all this set with seemingly consummate abandon against the immaculate azure of the purest blue sky, immeasurable in its depth, fathomless in its beauty. And I had leisure to take all this in, for the anger of the crowd, like the swell of a restless sea, took time to subside. But at length it was quiet enough for me to make myself heard; and when they realised that I was speaking in Aramaic, the gathering fell completely silent. I took a deep breath, and launched into a detailed account of my origin, upbringing and experiences. All went well until I spoke of my call to take the Good News to Gentiles. The word had scarcely dropped from my lips when the riot erupted again with redoubled fervour. With chilling spontaneity the sea of upturned faces before me was convulsed with virulent hatred. No longer could I savour the vivid loveliness I had drunk in so gratefully only minutes earlier – the air was grey with thick dust, and filled with violently flapping cloaks; and the noise was deafening.

The commander lost patience. "Bring him inside," he barked. I was hustled into the barrack yard. "Stretch him out." Almost before I grasped what was about to happen, my clothes were ripped from my back, two burly soldiers grabbed my arms, and I was tied by the wrists to two wooden posts set in the paving stones. With malicious pleasure, a third man slowly picked up a vicious-looking lash, fixing my eye with a small, meaningful smile as he did so. He moved behind me. I heard a small intake of breath. "You've been through this before, haven't you?" I nodded, weakly. "So you know what to expect then, don't you?" I saw the centurion in charge incline his head slightly to his subordinate. The man moved back a step, and raised his flogging arm over his head. I mustered my wits. "Can you legally flog a man who is a Roman citizen," I asked the centurion, "and moreover has not been found guilty?" The effect of my intervention was dramatic. The centurion ordered the soldier to lower his arm. He turned on his heel and went into the commander's room. The two of them came out together, and the commander asked if I was really a Roman citizen. I assured him I was. "It cost me a large sum to acquire this citizenship," he said. "But it was mine by birth," I replied. A muttered imprecation escaped his lips, and he personally untied the thongs holding me to the posts. I was kept in the fortress overnight – "solely for your own safety, you understand" – and next morning I was escorted to an official meeting with the Sanhedrin, which the commander said he had summoned because he needed to understand clearly what underlay the previous day's disturbance. I suspect he was more baffled at the end of the proceedings than he had been at the beginning. Invited to make my own case to the meeting, I had spoken precisely one sentence when, to my utter disbelief, Ananias the High Priest ordered me to be struck across the mouth. Instantly a stinging slap cracked across my face, opening a cut on my upper lip. Within seconds the bittersweet taste of warm blood invaded my mouth. My self control snapped. Livid with rage, I swore at Ananias. "God will strike you, you whitewashed wall! You sit there to judge me in accordance with the law; and then in defiance of the law you order me to be struck!" I had barely released the words before I desperately wished that I could recall them. A gasp of horror swept the assembly, and one of the attendants asked me, in tones of shocked incredulity, "Would you insult God's High Priest?" Scarcely able myself to believe what I had done, I mumbled the lamest possible excuse, to the effect that I had no idea that he was the High Priest. I groaned inwardly as it dawned on me that I had done my case the maximum damage possible, and that my only hope of salvaging anything from such a comprehensive debâcle was to adopt a completely different approach – and in the same instant I became aware of a golden opportunity right there, staring me full in the face. "My brothers, I am a Pharisee," I called out, "a Pharisee born and bred; and the true issue in this trial is our hope of the resurrection of the dead."

Though I say it myself, it was a masterstroke. It cut as clean as a cleaver through the opposition ranged against me. I could almost have been amused by the way in which the two dominant groups in the Sanhedrin instantly fell to berating and mauling each other, the

Pharisees suddenly discovering that I was not so much in the wrong after all, while the Saducees, who reject any idea of resurrection, hotly insisted that I had condemned myself out of my own mouth. Not that the fratricidal strife in the assembly left me immune to violence – once again I found myself in the middle of a mêlée, pushed and pulled, this way and that, until I was actually relieved to see Roman soldiers bearing down upon me to rescue me from the frantic frenzy of my co-religionists. There followed another night in the safety of a cell in the fortress; and in the state of heightened tension still hanging in the air, I was not at all surprised to see Jesus again, and to hear him say, "Keep up your courage; you have affirmed the truth about Me in Jerusalem, and you must do the same in Rome." Unexpectedly, the vision and the words brought me deep peace. I knew perfectly well that disturbances outside the Council chamber and dissension within it had resolved nothing. My presence and my preaching in Jerusalem were obviously inflammatory; but while all around me were undeniably in varying states of agitation, I experienced calm and stillness. I had longed to go to Rome; now the Living Lord himself had answered my dearest hope. I found myself able to let go of all my cares and concerns, in the unruffled assurance that his will would be done, whatever the means he might choose to achieve it. *[Acts 23:11]*

And the means matched the mood of the moment. There was a knock next morning at the door of my room. Before I could answer, a Roman soldier came in with a slightly-built teenager. "Do you know this young man, sir?" he enquired. I jumped up in delight. "Know him?" I echoed, "Know him? Of course I know him – he's my sister's only boy! Well, how are you, lad?" I embraced him warmly. "What brings you to see your old uncle here, eh?" He gave me a small basket of fresh fruit, but was obviously unwilling to speak while the soldier was still in the room; so I nodded, and the soldier left. Only then did the boy speak, at first in an urgent whisper. "Uncle," he said, "I've heard a really worrying rumour. A friend of a friend of mine says he overheard a group of men in the Temple precinct talking about taking an oath not to eat or drink until they've" – he hesitated, and looked anxiously at me – "until they've killed you." I gulped inwardly, but tried to take the news calmly. "They have asked the chief priests to request that you be brought before the Council again – and they will make sure that you never arrive." My mind raced for a few moments. Then I called the duty centurion. "Take this young man to the commander," I said; "he has something to report." From then on developments unfolded at an accelerating rate. That night was still and quiet, and I was just beginning to think of turning in, when two centurions entered my room. "We leave now for Caesarea," one of them said. "Commander's orders. I understand you know the reason why." There was neither need nor opportunity for questions or objections. Rolling up my few belongings in my mat, I followed them out of the room. I was completely taken aback at the sight that greeted my eyes. The entire parade ground of Fortress Antonia was packed with nigh on five hundred troops – infantry, cavalry, spearmen – all drawn up in close order and all, apart from the occasional whinny of a horse, or the clatter of harness as a hoof moved on a paving stone, utterly silent. Light from torches in brackets on the walls round the yard reflected off gleaming breastplates, and lent an eerie air to motionless faces half seen, half hidden in the shadow of close-fitting helmets. It was an astonishing spectacle, an awe-inspiring demonstration of disciplined might, all the more impressive for being so totally unexpected. I was led to a small string of riderless horses right in the middle of the company, and expertly hoisted onto the back of one of them. The officer in charge and his subordinates mounted the others, and on a hand-given signal each line in turn wheeled and moved under the archway, out onto the empty streets of the city, and through the Damascus Gate into the moon-lit hills that slowly dropped down to the coastal plain towards Caesarea. At first I imagined that previously arranged troop manoeuvres were being utilised to get me out of harm's way; but this theory fell to the ground when we reached Antipatris, where the infantry about turned, and marched all the way back to Jerusalem. I wondered if the whole exercise had been an elaborate feint to tempt suspected conspirators to show their hand – but of course I had no way of finding out. The cavalry, with me still in their midst, went on to Caesarea, where I appeared briefly before Antonius Felix, the Roman Procurator. He was reading a letter when I was shown into his presence; it was obvious that it related to me, but he deferred my case until, as he said, "Your accusers arrive."

Five days later they duly arrived. I was almost flattered that even Ananias the High Priest had put himself to the trouble of travelling to Caesarea to testify against me; but strangely, all of the tension that had been so dramatically generated in Jerusalem in the previous week, now just drained away. Counsel for the prosecution made an opening speech, and I was allowed to reply. I reiterated the basic fact which I had proclaimed earlier in Athens, and had then repeated to such good effect just a week earlier in Jerusalem – "The true issue in my trial before you today is the resurrection of the dead." But Felix lowered the temperature all round by adjourning my case, and placing me under a very relaxed house arrest. I was fairly certain that this was because he was surprisingly well informed about the Way, and even, I suspected, well disposed towards it. For a while I found myself in a situation very similar to the stories I had heard about John the Baptist – like him, I was regularly sent for by my captor, for discussions on religious and moral issues; and like John's captor, Felix was sensitive on the subject of his relationship with his partner Drusilla, whom he had enticed from her husband, King Azizus of Emesa. At the same time, I enjoyed talking with this intelligent, sympathetic man; but weeks lengthened into months, and eventually two whole years elapsed with no progress in my case. Ultimately I began to wonder if the Procurator was deliberately delaying matters in the hope that I would ease things along with a bribe; but if that was the case, he was disappointed when he was moved on from his post.

I was disappointed too, to be left still languishing in custody. <u>Felix</u> was succeeded as Procurator by <u>Porcius Festus</u>. It was hardly possible to miss the rumpus in the town when he arrived at Caesarea; but of course, he was only passing through on his way to Jerusalem. Even so, it was less than a fortnight before he was back in Caesarea to hear my case. I heard on the grapevine that the Jewish leaders had urged him to send for me to be brought back to Jerusalem – presumably so that they could mount an ambush against me on the way. I was profoundly grateful to him for refusing their malicious request. So my hearing was resumed in Caesarea. I had no difficulty in rebutting firmly all the groundless charges brought against me by my opponents, but Festus, anxious to make a good impression on his new subjects, casually asked me if I would consent to be tried in Jerusalem. Aware of what lay behind this suggestion, I pointed out that I was standing before the Emperor's tribunal, not the Jewish Sanhedrin. Weary now with the whole long drawn out business of incarceration and investigation, I decided to seize the initiative in an attempt to move things along. Exercising my indisputable rights as a Roman citizen, I took a deep breath and called out in open court, "I appeal to Caesar." The reaction was fascinating to observe. Initial consternation on the faces of my opponents rapidly gave way to rage as they realised that I would not now be within their reach. Festus' face betrayed no emotion. One eyebrow rose slightly as he turned to consult his advisors; then he simply stated, "You have appealed to Caesar: to Caesar you shall go."

It proved naïve of me to have hoped that by appealing to Caesar I would be able to expedite my case. I was returned to house arrest, and left there for some time, until the next local excitement came along. This took the form of an official visit to Festus by King Herod Agrippa II and his sister Bernice. I had the distinct impression that I was a welcome diversion for the host – I was brought before his guests as something more or less half way between an entertainment and a polite request for professional advice. It was mildly interesting to observe all the goings on connected with a state function. It must have taken half the morning for the king and his entourage to get themselves arrayed in all their finery. Silks and satins were as plentiful as camel hair and goat skins in a tentmaker's shop; rings and bangles and armlets and neck chains vied with each other in flashing reflected light, exotic perfumes hung heavily in the air, and elaborate hairstyles were topped with much over decorated headdresses – the unaffected simplicity of white Roman togas, edged where appropriate with restrained purple, stood out in sharp contrast as silent statements of good taste. The occasion generated no dramatic tension – in no sense was I on trial, as I had been previously; but it was another opportunity to proclaim the Good News of Jesus, and I did my best to make the most of it. I had spoken in crowded market places and busy streets, in attentive synagogues and on peaceful river banks, I had known quiet listening and raucous heckling – now I had for a while the ear of the politically powerful and the socially significant. I was heard for quite a while in respectful silence; but suddenly I knew I had pierced the veneer of mere good manners. No sooner had I revealed the heart of the matter, with the proclamation of the resurrection of Jesus Christ from the dead, than the Enemy was stung to attack. Without any hint of forewarning, the Procurator suddenly leapt to his feet and bawled out something to the effect that I was raving – that too much study had driven me mad. There was a moment of awkward silence. On an impulse I made a direct appeal to King Agrippa – it was widely known that he, like Festus' immediate predecessor, the Procurator Felix, was well-informed about the Way. "Do you believe the prophets?" I challenged him; "I know you do." It was not my most astute move. The king, already embarrassed by his host's strange outburst, made a suitably enigmatic reply, and brought the proceedings to an abrupt end by rising from his seat. The rest of the company had perforce to stand as well, and the royal party swept grandly out of the hall, with the discomfited Roman Procurator scurrying along beside them, anxiously attempting to repair the damage his behaviour had done. It eventually filtered back to me that the upshot of the subsequent private discussion between Festus and his guests was that I had done nothing deserving of death or even imprisonment, and that if I had not appealed to Caesar, I could have been discharged.

But I had appealed to Caesar; and so, stultifyingly slowly, the wheels began to turn, to give effect to my decision. I was put in the charge of a centurion named Julius, along with some other prisoners, and we were placed on board a ship bound for Asia. A day's sailing brought us to Sidon, where I was allowed to leave the ship to stay overnight with friends in the town. When I re-embarked, I sensed a very slight uncertainty among the crew; but we weighed anchor, and beat steadily northwards, tacking against an equally steady north-west wind. It became obvious that the captain was steering for maximum advantage from offshore winds – we first sailed east of Cyprus, and then north of it; but eventually we lost the benefit of the leeward coast, and had to head due west, out into the open sea. I have never been seasick; but other people were not so fortunate, and the pitch and roll of the ship as she butted her way through an unrelenting head wind had predictable consequences for those poor souls. At our next port of call we were transferred to a vessel sailing for Italy with corn from Egypt; but progress against the prevailing north-westerly was frustratingly slow. The captain hugged the coast as closely as he dared; but deep bays and inlets, and the many small islands off the coast, made navigation very tricky. In the end he decided that he could not afford to lose any more time, so he abandoned the protection of the mainland, and set a south-westerly course for Crete. This time he judged that the southern coast of the island would afford us greater safety, with less danger of being blown onto the rocks, and perhaps even the possibility of picking up a local southerly wind. But we still made infuriatingly slow progress; the cliffs and hills of Crete to starboard seemed to be maddeningly immobile, despite the crew's unremitting efforts to extract every inch of advantage from the contrary wind. Then when we finally reached Fair Havens the captain pronounced the harbour there to be unsuitable for wintering in. At that point I summoned up enough courage to put my own figurative oar in. I aired my opinion that as we were now well into the Autumn, it could be courting disaster to attempt to go any further; but I was virtually a lone voice – the general consensus was that we should try to get at least as far as the south-west corner of Crete. I could not help noticing that the very slight uncertainty I had earlier sensed among the previous ship's crew had strengthened into palpable unease on the part of the sailors working the vessel we were now on – an unease which was only slightly mollified when, almost as if to order, a welcome southerly breeze suddenly sprang up. The owner of the ship, who was on board with us, used the fact to press home to the captain his argument that we should sail on while we could, in the hope of making up some at least of the time we had already lost. The captain was markedly reluctant to go along with the idea, but did so in the end – in the last analysis, of course, he had no choice.

The next morning dawned clear and bright. To me, a mere landlubber, it seemed too bright for the time of year. Nevertheless, we nosed out of the inlet where we had dropped anchor for the night, and set a westerly course. Very soon, however, thin high-level cloud began to reduce the brightness of the sunlight. It thickened steadily, until well before noon the sun was completely obscured. Then, ominously, the southerly breeze suddenly dropped. The sea, which had been running a slight swell, inexplicably began to bump a bit, and from dreamy blue it quickly changed to unfriendly grey. The captain ordered all canvas to be spread, in a desperate attempt to extract the last drop of advantage for the becalmed vessel. And then the wind struck. It didn't get up – it bore down. With no forewarning that I could detect, there was a low distant moan from the direction of the mountains of Crete to starboard. The sails flapped briefly, almost as if taken by surprise; but in next to no time at all they were first billowing in flexible rhythm, and then bulging with rigid roundness, as they took the full force of a fierce north-easterly gale. The ship gathered speed at a rate which jolted unsecured tackle to the stern, and sent experienced crewmen and unwary passengers alike scrabbling for something to hold on to. The captain shouted himself red in the face, but the wind whipped his words away almost before he uttered them. Maybe he was screaming at the crew to turn the ship's head into the wind; but they could no more do that than they could hear his orders, so they simply did the most urgently needed thing in the circumstances – they struck the mainsail in order to reduce the risk of capsizing. The ship was now positively careering ahead, but still being buffeted severely by the rapidly rising waves. The boat was being flung against the stern as if it was a mere child's toy, so it was hauled aboard and secured; as a possible last means of escape, it was vital that it should not be damaged in any way.

Almost all non-crew personnel were by now below decks, most of them moaning on their mats before vomiting on the floor. The sights and sounds and smells were so revolting that I was profoundly grateful for my own sea legs, and spent all my time on deck. The noise of the wind was terrifying – it was a sustained wail, sometimes rising in a crescendo of sound, but somehow never seeming to abate in volume. Even more alarming was the audible protest of the ship at the brutal way in which it was being treated. The timbers of the hull creaked and groaned under the pressures they were being subjected to; so, in an undertaking of equal skill and danger, the crew frapped the ship by passing heavy-duty ropes under the hull, and tightening them on a windlass. Needless to say, the helm had to be continuously manned; but for most of the time it seemed to be a totally ineffectual exercise – we were wholly at the mercy of elements over which we had no control. At first we assumed that we were caught up in a short burst of fury which would quickly pass; but the storm showed no sign of abating – if anything, it seemed to be gaining in intensity. There was no sleep for anyone that night – nor, apart from brief snatches from sheer exhaustion, for several more nights to come. After forty-eight hours of this relentless battering, the captain gave orders for all non-essential equipment to be jettisoned. It made not a smidgen of difference. Huge waves reared up astern, some of them almost tipping the ship vertical on her bows, others crashing over her in a terrifying torrent of rushing water, temporarily submerging her, until we felt we would never resurface. All the time the wind was screaming through the rigging; and we saw nothing but surging grey water, topped with ragged white spume racing madly from wave-crest to wave-crest. There was no horizon – the grey sea merged inseparably with grey clouds scudding low across the sky; and as if we weren't wet enough from drenching waves and flying spray, pitiless rain drilled down on us from time to time, leaving us soaked to the skin, and shivering with cold.

And then, unbelievably, in the midst of all the shouting and shuddering and shaking, a pool of white light, still and silent, materialised, and a voice, calm and clear, said, "Do not be afraid, Paul. It is ordained that you shall appear before the Emperor; and be assured, God has granted you the lives of all who are sailing with you." Just that. Nothing more – but nothing less. The storm continued for a full fortnight, with no sign of any let up; but eventually older, more experienced, crew members began to sniff the air and scan the horizon. It seems they had sensed some indefinable difference in the movement of the swell. They dropped a line and sounded twenty fathoms. A second sounding a short while later yielded only fifteen fathoms. Suddenly the whole atmosphere on board changed. With newly charged energy, sailors raced to the stern and cast four anchors. Then they lowered the ship's boat. When I asked why, I was told they were going to lay out anchors from the bows. I had enough experience of sailing to know that it made no sense at all to try to anchor the ship in that depth of water, under cover of darkness, in those weather conditions. It dawned on me that an escape attempt was being made right under our noses. I decided to intervene. I told Julius what was happening. His men promptly cut the ropes holding the boat. It disappeared into the darkness, and we hardly heard the splash it made as it hit the water, above the whistling of the wind and the turmoil of the sea. Strangely, that act raised the level of hope on board. I seized the opportunity to boost morale further. At daybreak I took some bread, and in front of the entire ship's complement, gave thanks to God for it, broke it, and began to eat. The effect was immediate and dramatic. The paralysing fear which had gripped no fewer than two hundred and seventy-six people for two whole weeks suddenly evaporated. Everyone joined in; and the rising level of confidence was highlighted when the passengers joined the crew in helping to dump the entire cargo of corn overboard.

Then the reluctant dawn revealed land ahead. None of the crew recognised it; but no one had time to gaze at it for long. Orders were being shouted out in rapid succession. The anchors at the stern were slipped and let go, the lashings securing the steering paddles were loosened, the foresail was set, and the ship began to drive relentlessly towards the shore. The end was almost predictable. There was a fearsome grating noise, and with the crew quite unable to control her, the ship's bow struck the beach with a force that threw everybody off their feet. And there she stuck, immovable, each succeeding wave only serving to embed her ever more deeply in the sand and shingle. Although we were in the relative shelter of a bay, huge breakers were still crashing on the beach; and the stern took a fearful pounding. After all the ship had been through already, it was hardly surprising that she began to break up. The escort party who had drawn their swords to thwart the sailors' earlier attempt to escape now unsheathed them again; and I realised with a cold stab of fear that this time it was me and my fellow prisoners that they intended to despatch, in case we should try to escape. The glint of naked steel transfixed me; but an urgent shout from the centurion saved our lives. His order came hardly a moment too soon. With a heart-stopping splintering of wood, the stern of the ship finally disintegrated. The planking of the deck where I was standing began to break up. Julius wasted no time on the courtesies of etiquette. Without waiting for the captain's command, he barked the order to abandon ship. There was a headlong dash for the bows. Those who could swim jumped straight into the seething foam. I slipped and slithered down one of the ropes hanging over the side. The very first wave I encountered completely submerged me. There was a furious roaring sound in my ears; I was knocked clean off my feet and, arms and legs flailing helplessly, I was swept bodily onto the beach, and unceremoniously dumped on cold, wet sand. The water ebbed away from me, and I was just able to summon the strength to crawl on hands and knees above the reach of the next wave as it curled over, broke, and at last spent its remaining energy in a futile rush against the rise of the beach.

XIII

OPPORTUNITY

"TWO hundred and seventy-three, two hundred and seventy-four." A bedraggled soldier moved to stand ram-rod straight in front of Julius. "Two hundred and seventy-five with yourself, sir," he announced. "Did you include yourself in your count?" the centurion asked. "Sorry sir, no, I didn't", the man replied. "Two hundred and seventy-six, then," Julius corrected him, turning to look at me with a mix of curiosity and respect. It was only then that we experienced the unsettling suspicion that we were being watched. As the sullen light grew unwillingly stronger, we became aware of forms crouching in the long grass on top of the low banks surrounding the bay. On a quick quiet order from the centurion, the soldiers formed a defensive semicircle round the rest of us; but as first one, then another, and another, of the threatening shapes in the long grass stood up and innocently waved to us, Julius stood his men down, and the tension relaxed. Some of the figures came down onto the beach, and made welcoming sounds and gestures. I was surprised at how relatively primitive they were in dress; but what they lacked in superficial sophistication, they more than made up in practical kindness – I was not the only one in our party to have a warm animal skin fur

> Acts 28:3 says the snake (ἔχιδνα) fastened itself to his hand
> in v. 4 uses τὸ θηρίον (wild beast).

placed round my shoulders. Rain had set in again, so we were only too glad to follow the native people off the wet and windswept beach, inland to a tree-sheltered enclosure. In the middle of a circle of poor huts a fire was flickering desultorily, so we set to, to make it more effective. I gathered up a whole armful of sticks from under the trees, and was throwing them onto the fire, when a snake slithered out from the heat and bit me. The local people's reactions gave their thoughts away; for the rest of the day they looked at me askance, and avoided any contact with me, clearly deducing that I must be a fugitive from the vengeance of the gods, who would not let me live, even though I had escaped from the storm at sea. Later I heard that when I was still alive and well next morning, they changed their minds – and not for the first time, I was mistaken for a god!

We made many good friends among the Maltese people during our three-month stay on their island. We enjoyed three days of generous hospitality from the island's chief magistrate, Publius, while more long-term arrangements were made to accommodate us for the rest of the winter; and although I received no more visions, I was given renewed assurance that God had not forsaken me when people who were ill were healed – including Publius' own father. Julius, however, had still not discharged his obligation to hand over his prisoners in Rome, and he warned us that as soon as Spring brought better weather, we would resume our journey. So it was that we eventually found ourselves on yet another ship; but this time we had an uneventful voyage, first to Sicily, then to southern Italy, and on to Puteoli, where I was not sorry to take my leave of ships and the sea. The change was made all the sweeter by the fact that there were fellow believers in the town who looked after us while Julius allowed us a week's respite from travelling.

I felt a growing sense of excitement when we resumed

our journey. At long last, after months of discomfort and danger, I was nearing the goal I had longed for for years – the opportunity to proclaim Christ in the capital city of the world's greatest Empire. My eager anticipation was heightened when, all unexpectedly, we met with Christians from Rome who had heard that we were coming, and had travelled out to meet us – it was immensely encouraging to be met with smiling faces, outstretched arms and warm embraces. And then we reached Rome – and Rome was a devastating disappointment. True, the first glimpse of the city in the distance was exciting enough – but closer acquaintance swiftly dispelled my fond illusions about it. It was possible to pick out the famous seven hills on which the city is built; but they were conspicuous only for a mass of unlovely buildings which sprawled all over them in unplanned confusion. The Appian Way, the fine paved road on which we approached the city, became steadily more thronged with people, animals and vehicles of all kinds as we got nearer, until it eventually plunged into a morass of narrow, dirty streets, so crowded, that it was sometimes next to impossible to move through them. We passed tenements of two, three, sometimes even more, storeys, some of them constructed entirely of wood – and the dreadful possible consequence of that was brought home to us when we came upon the burnt-out shell of a building that must have caught fire only a few hours earlier – charred timbers were still smoking, and a long straggle of exhausted looking men were passing pitifully small leather buckets of water up the line, to damp down smouldering embers. But the architecture and the construction of the buildings both improved dramatically when we finally reached the city centre; columns, arches, temples, baths in fine white stone glistened on all sides in brilliant sunlight from a sapphire sky – by the time we reached the quarters of the Praetorian Guard I was sated with sightseeing, and weary with walking. But then I had a pleasant surprise – I was taken to a small house nearby, and told that I would be lodged there, with just one soldier to guard me. This was very much better treatment than I could ever have expected. I wondered if Julius had put in a good word for me – he and I had come to respect and like each other during the four months or so since we had first made each other's acquaintance in Caesarea; and as an officer in an Augustan Cohort, Julius would certainly have been able to exercise some influence.

I decided to test just how far I was free to act. I succeeded in making contact with some of the leaders of the Jewish community, which was just beginning to grow again after the Edict of Expulsion issued by Claudius some ten years earlier. I introduced myself to them, but was somewhat deflated to be told that they knew nothing about me, good or bad; but they agreed that they would like to know what my views were, adding rather worryingly, "All we know about this sect is that no one has a good word to say for it." This, then, was clearly a challenge for me. We agreed a date and time for a meeting, and I was pleasantly surprised by the large number who turned up. I gave all I had to that opportunity. From soon after dawn to just before dusk, I talked and listened and explained and argued; but I ended the day disappointed, as well as exhausted. There was much spirited discussion, between individuals, and in groups, and some people professed themselves convinced; but more remained sceptical. As much in exasperation as in sadness, I quoted damning words of indictment from Isaiah – 'You will hear and hear, but never understand; you will look and look, but never see. For this people has grown gross at heart; their ears are dull, and their eyes are closed. Otherwise, their eyes might see, their ears hear, and their heart understand, and then they might turn again, and I would heal them.' I heard myself saying once again what I had said on more than one occasion previously – "This salvation of God has been sent to the Gentiles; the Gentiles will listen."

There followed two years of comfortable uncertainty. The conditions of my detention were so light as to be barely noticeable, apart from restrictions on travelling, and my days were full of interest as a steady stream of visitors called to enquire, to encourage, and to enthuse me. One in particular I was deeply touched by – though he presented me with a really thorny dilemma. One warm sunny morning there was a knock at the street door. As usual, my guard went to open it, and was followed back into the room by a once fine-looking young man who had clearly fallen on bad times. His aquiline features were gaunt, his deep dark eyes sunk into his thin face, his straight back visible through holes and tears in his threadbare tunic – but I still recognised him. He was a slave whom I had first met in the household of *Philemon at Ephesus; and I remembered his name, as well – Onesimus. In the nick of time, however, I just managed to check myself from greeting him by name – if I had given his identity away to my guard, who knows what chain of links might have connected him to his master, now living in Colossae, with the consequent possibility of all the savage cruelties reserved for captured runaway slaves being inflicted on this sensitive, intelligent individual? So I gave no sign of recognition until the soldier had left the room – and then Onesimus sank to his knees and promptly broke down in floods of tears. I realised that he was reacting to the sudden lifting of months of stress and strain, and the relief of seeing a face he knew, and of meeting someone to whom he could unburden himself. And that is exactly what happened. I sat silent, letting the storm of released emotion blow itself out; and eventually he began to talk. In between slowly subsiding bursts of sobbing he poured out, first hesitantly,

*Some would hold that this meeting took place in Ephesus, where Onesimus and Paul were both in prison.

then with increasing frankness, everything that had happened to him since we last met. The top and the bottom of it was that he had run away from his master, had made his way to Rome, as nearly all of them did, and was now at his wits' end. Going back was out of the question – he knew, or thought he knew, exactly what awaited him if he did that; but neither could he see any way forward. I listened. I listened many times, and came to develop a warm affection for this young man, seemingly washed up at my door by the random tide of life's unfeeling ebbs and flows. Soon he was willing to listen as well as talk, and eventually we reached the point where he responded for himself to the Good News of Jesus the Saviour.

But that then opened up another problem for him. He realised that his commitment to the Way inevitably entailed an upward revision of his personal attitudes and standards. We entered a period of grappling together with the unpalatable fact of the need for his return to his master, Philemon. Here, though, I was able to be of practical help. I reminded Onesimus that Philemon was himself a Christian; and I undertook to write a letter asking him to take his runaway slave back, and to treat him more as a fellow believer than as an errant wrongdoer. Onesimus took a deal more persuading; but in the end he promised me that he would deliver my letter to his master in person. It was with very mixed emotions that I watched him walk slowly down to the corner of the street. He turned and lifted his hand in final farewell. I committed him fervently to the grace of God; but not to this day do I know the upshot of that brave act of faith.

I had written quite a few letters before that one to Philemon. Increasingly I have found myself drawn to write letters by the pull of events. There have been developments of doctrine to be expounded, problems with people to be resolved, misunderstandings and errors to be rectified. I have written to churches I founded, to encourage and stimulate them; I have written to churches I have never even visited, to explain myself to them, or to warn them against dangerous distortions of the revelation I had received. I have written private letters to individuals, and general letters for circulation to groups of churches. As the years have gone by I have realised that there are more and more churches I will never be able to visit – my long-cherished hope of travelling to Spain, for example, to meet believers there, has steadily receded over the horizon; so I have devoted my energies instead to making as much use as possible of the opportunities for communication presented by quill and parchment, amanuensis and messenger.

The processes involved in actually bringing me to the Emperor's tribunal seemed to drag out interminably; and when at last I finally stood there, in front of Nero himself, the whole thing collapsed in anticlimax. Unshaven, he slouched into the cool marble audience chamber, looking suspiciously as if the effects of the night before had not yet worn off; he took one perfunctory glance at me from half-glazed eyes under heavy lids, and then appeared to slump into slumber while the history of my case was read out in meticulous detail by an obsequious court official. I was surprised to be allowed no chance at all of speaking in my own defence, in striking contrast to all the hearings I had been given in inferior courts; but I was much more unsettled by the fact that on the day fixed for my appearance in court no one was there to support me – not one. The only people in the room were those directly involved. I ruefully reflected that I had apparently made no impact at all where I had most wanted to – in the very heart of the Empire itself. My case aroused no interest whatsoever, even among people I thought were friends and sympathisers – not even in Caesar himself. At the end of all the submissions and statements and legal procedures, Nero roused himself sufficiently to say "Case not proven – release the prisoner. Next!" To my astonishment I found myself a free man again.

Nevertheless, it is becoming steadily more obvious to me that my time in this life is inexorably running out. There are the only to be expected indicators of physical deterioration – my eyesight has worsened to the point where even to sign my own name requires bigger and bigger letters each time, if I am to see what I am writing; and I feel the cold now as I never used to. To my chagrin I discovered that I left the one really warm cloak I ever possessed at Troas, when I stayed there with Carpus. I have written to Timothy, asking him to pick it up and bring it with him when he comes to see me; but winter is approaching fast, and I fear he will not get here before the cold weather does. At any other time this would not have been a problem at all – any number of people would, I know, have provided me with plenty of warm clothing. But my circumstances have changed now. A major fire broke out in Rome a few weeks ago. No fewer than fourteen wards of the city were devastated. A lurid red glow lit up the sky all night long, and a pall of thick smoke hung over the city for the whole of the next day. Bewildered and angry citizens fanned a rumour that the fire had been started deliberately by the Emperor, to clear land for a pet building project of his; and so many people were made homeless that the government thought it politic to try and fix blame for the disaster on a small but easily identifiable unpopular group in the community. On these criteria the Christians as good as selected themselves; and along with scores of my fellow believers, I have been arrested and imprisoned on a wholly fictitious charge of arson. The conditions of my incarceration now could not be more different from those of my previous detention. I am in solitary confinement in a dark, dank and dirty cell, where the only light filters through a grating high up on one wall. I barely have freedom to move now; I am permanently chained to one of four soldiers in turn, who are responsible for me on a rotating basis. They must have been ordered to have no dealings with me whatsoever – I have tried all the approaches I can think of to communicate with them, but I get not the faintest flicker of response from any of them. So I am reduced to observing them, and thinking.

As there is virtually nothing else to focus on, I have been concentrating on what they are wearing. It is obvious that it is all subordinated to the one overriding requirement of fitness for purpose – a soldier wears nothing that will not either help him to defend himself under attack, or make him as effective as possible when he is ordered to go on to the offensive. I can see a parallel there with my life as a Christian believer – the more I can discard clogging trivia, the more useful I shall be in the struggle with cosmic powers, the authorities and potentates of this dark world, the superhuman forces of evil in the heavens. What strikes me first as I contemplate my guard is the fact that all his clothing is kept in place by his belt. There is potent symbolism in that – there must be something which keeps all else under control, a defining, governing principle, to impose order, and to maintain it. I can think of nothing more fundamental than the fact of truth – but not truth as philosophers and moralists and ethicisers think of it, an abstraction, a concept, a subjective relativism, blown to and fro by whatever wind of fashion or whim of fancy may happen along at any time. No, I have long been held captive by the insight John opened up to me when we first met in Jerusalem, all those years ago, and began exploring each other's experience and understanding of Jesus. John spoke of him as being full of truth. He told me that one of the very few statements Jesus had made when he was on trial for his life was "My task is to bear witness to the truth. For this was I born; for this I came into the world, and all who are not deaf to truth listen to My voice." Apparently the then Procurator, Pontius Pilate, had asked, whether in contempt or bafflement John could not say, "What is truth?" But John went on to share with me something Jesus had said earlier, which not only answered Pilate's later question, but has proved to be for me the conclusive definition of truth, the ultimate understanding of it, the central core of its reality. In answer to a question from Thomas on the previous evening, at their last meal together, Jesus had simply said, "I am the truth." So I came to see that truth is in essence not a proposition, but a Person, and that all true Christian belief and behaviour must be subject, not to a thinker's theory, but to a Living Lord – it must be contained within the constraints of a real relationship with the Risen Redeemer.

I look at my guard again. His uniform, under the overall control of his belt, provides protection for him – he wears a coat of mail. I reflect that the need for defensive clothing bespeaks weakness; and that suggests another powerful parallel to me. In all conscience I have been aware of weakness, other people's, as well as my own – indeed, everyone's weakness. I recall putting the idea in different ways in some of the letters I have written to various churches. In fact, I remember writing to the Christians here in this very city of Rome itself, "For all alike have sinned, and are deprived of the divine splendour"; and it is a lethal weakness – "It was through one man that sin entered the world, and through sin, death, and thus death pervaded the whole human race, inasmuch as all have sinned." We are all in desperate need of a spiritual coat of mail; and it must be of an effectiveness which will more than compensate for the deadly weakness which flaws us all, Jew and Gentile, believer and non-believer. The picture has come to me before, and now it presents itself to me again, with added force. Just as the soldier wakes from sleep and puts on his coat of mail, so the believer, emerging from baptism into the new day of endless life, has 'put on' Christ, and his righteousness. Nothing less will avail to make good our fatal weakness. I am vividly reminded of Isaiah's trenchant comment – "All our righteous deeds are like a filthy rag." Filthy rags will be of no use at all in covering the soldier's weakness in the cut and thrust of combat. By analogy, believers will be mortally vulnerable unless they are clothed with the perfect righteousness made available to them by God in his own Child Jesus.

There is the sound of footsteps at the door. Bolts are drawn back, and the door creaks noisily open. Never a word is spoken, but my guard for the last six hours is freed from the manacles chaining him to me by his replacement, who is then himself fettered by the man going off duty. The iron door clangs to, and bolts are rammed home with unnecessary force. Footsteps recede. It must be afternoon. There is enough light filtering through the small grill for me to be able to contemplate my new guardian. His dress is identical to that of his predecessor; and my attention is drawn to the footwear which first announced his coming. He has regulation army issue boots on his feet. I have never previously made particularly detailed observations of army boots; but now I am grateful for anything which will stimulate my mind. I try to think of ways of including a soldier's footwear in my extended parable. This one is difficult. My captor is wearing boots with leather soles and uppers, and thonging halfway up his calves. They are clearly designed for marching for miles along the well-paved arrow-straight roads steadily spreading all over the Empire – I utilised them myself in my travelling days; and that recollection gives me a point of reference. Soldiers' boots facilitate war and conquest; they are used for tramping to new places and foreign parts, and too often for trampling callously and cruelly on helpless people and their deepest needs. But then words from Isaiah's prophecy come to my mind: 'How lovely on the mountains are the feet of the herald who comes to proclaim prosperity and bring good news, the news of deliverance'. I see a complete reversal of rôles here. Believers' feet must serve the purpose, not of subjugation, but of liberation, by bringing the Good News of peace to the downtrodden and oppressed – first and foremost peace with God through Jesus Christ; and then as a result of that, and building on it, peace with each other, and peace with ourselves. I have had sufficient experience of life now to know that only the peace of God, which is of far more worth than human reasoning, can provide footing firm enough for us to stand our ground when things are at their worst – to complete every task, and still to stand.

Now what little light there is is beginning to fade; but over in the corner of my cell I can still see the shield my guard put there when he came on duty. It is a stout construction of leather strips overlaying each other, braced with a wooden frame and a brass boss at the centre. It gleams dully in the encircling gloom, and I know why – I have often seen soldiers in barracks assiduously oiling their shields to keep them pliable and waterproof. His shield is a soldier's most flexible means of self-defence, light enough for him to carry on his arm, and to move instantly to parry any attack, from whatever direction it might come. This analogy is easy for me – it as good as chooses itself. The believer's shield is his faith, his total trust in God. Provided he uses it, he can ward off everything the Enemy can throw at him – the blow of the cudgel, the slash of the sword, even arrows flaming with fire; nothing can penetrate the shield of the believer's faith. But it has to be permanently in place, and continuously maintained. No matter how conscientiously my soldier may oil his shield, it will be of no use at all to him left standing against the wall – he is as vulnerable as if he had no shield at all. I am struck by the need, not merely to keep my faith in tip-top condition, but to use it, at all times, and in all places; for I can never know when, or where, or how, I shall be under attack.

My attention wanders back to my guard. One of the most striking features of his armour is his helmet. It is made of metal, and fits his head closely, to provide maximum protection. Perhaps it is the most important defensive item he wears – if his head is injured, he is certain to be unable to carry on fighting. The parallel presents itself vividly to me. The most significant gift Christians are given is salvation itself. This is the foundation and fountain of all else they receive – truth, righteousness, peace, faith, all spring from the fundamental fact of salvation. Through all the years of my preaching, and in all the places to which I have travelled, this has been the core and content of my message – that <u>salvation is nothing less than a completely new creation, bestowed on us by God as the crown and consummation of our human existence</u>, the full and final realisation of the purpose for which we are made.

My silent sentinel suddenly sits, and his sword clangs noisily on the floor. I realise that it is the only offensive weapon with which he is equipped – but it is for that very reason the most potent. That sets me thinking again. Like the Roman soldier, the Christian believer is well provided with much needed defences against the adversary; but if the war is to be carried into the enemy's camp, he needs a means of attack as well. I have plenty of time – too much time – to reflect on this. Unlike soldiers, believers are not enlisted to fight human foes; rather, we are called to combat wicked spiritual forces in the heavenly world, where virulent evil rampages, seemingly unchecked. How can weak, puny creatures such as we even hope to defeat powers of such daunting malevolence and might? Clearly we need a sword – but a sword matched to the immensity of the task it must be put to. Is there anything in all the universe that can measure up to such a demand? The word 'universe' sparks a train of thought in my mind. The whole created order came into being by the agency of one instrument – the Word of God. Surely that which alone was powerful enough to create will alone be powerful enough to destroy. So even weak, puny creatures such as we can be more than conquerors if we take up <u>the sword the Spirit gives us – the Word of God</u>. But what exactly is the Word of God?

I take time to sit back, to try to take stock of who I am, what I have, and what I can do. I let my mind drift slowly back over the long vista of the decades that have elapsed since I was first captured by Christ. It seems to me now that the most effective weapon in my hands has been words – countless words spoken and innumerable words written; but above all, the Word heard, and received, and experienced, and obeyed. And my memory turns again to those priceless precious times in Jerusalem with John, who immeasurably developed my understanding of Jesus of Nazareth. I remember how he introduced me to the concept of Jesus as the Word of God, how he led me to realise that all the words written about God, and all the words spoken by God, stored up for us in the Scriptures, are ultimately brought to their full meaning in The Word of God, the Logos of the Greeks, the Messiah of the Jews – Jesus, in Whom dwells all the fullness of God.

The key turns in the lock again. I am jerked rudely out of my meditation. Surely it is not six hours since my guard was last changed? The newcomer nods almost imperceptibly in my direction; and with never a word spoken, I am suddenly yanked roughly to my feet, and without warning half pulled, half pushed, out of my cell, along the stone corridor outside, and up a winding staircase. At the top, keys clang again, and I am propelled through more passages and rooms. After days in the darkness of the dungeon, I am dazzled by the light of the dawn; but I am aware of curious stares from onlookers, and then suddenly, after the opening of yet another door, across a vast expanse of gleaming marble floor, I can just make out the figure of Nero, seated, with Senators and sycophants standing around. I am marched closer to him. The contrast with my recollection of him at our previous meeting could hardly be greater. He is clean shaven, clearly spoken, cold-eyed. I suspect that this time I am not here to be tried, but to be sentenced. I find myself curiously detached from what is happening all around me. I realise that I am in greater peril of my life than I have ever been before; and yet I am strangely unafraid – almost elated. I look steadfastly at my judge, and the scene dissolves. The hard face of Nero is eclipsed by a glow of glory, a glory I have seen before. A wreath of fading laurel leaves is transfigured into a golden crown of life; and I am content. Above and beyond the judgement seat there stands another door. In ecstasy, I mount the staircase leading to it. It opens of its own accord, and the splendour of the new unclouded day bursts upon my sight. Etched in brilliant white light is a down-pointing sword, unmistakably both sword and cross. The hour for my departure is upon me. I have fought the good fight. I have run the great race. I have finished the course. I have kept the faith.